This novel is a work of fiction. Any references to real events, businesses, organizations, and political figures are intended to give the story a sense of reality and authenticity. Any resemblance to actual private persons, living or dead, is entirely coincidental.

The Unwilling Recruit

Book design by Keith Katsikas

Cover design by Keith Katsikas

ISBN 978-1-9160418-0-6 (Paperback)

ISBN 948-1-9160418-1-3 (eBook)

1st Edition May 2017

2nd Edition March 2019

www.johnevansauthor.com

DEDICATION-

This book is dedicated to my son, Nathaniel.
I hope that, one day, you get as much pleasure out
of reading this as I have had in its writing.

All my love.

Dad xx

> *"I am he that liveth, and was dead; and behold, I am alive for evermore."*

Book of Revelations 1:18
King James Bible.

Chapter 1

The desert air was thick with acrid smoke. Hot, billowing clouds that appeared to have a life of their own. The ground erupted, throwing sand and dust into the air. All around, the sights and sounds of chaos. This was war, a place where man and machine pitted their skills against one another.

Soldiers scurried across the battlefield as they tried desperately to find the optimum position for victory. The screams of the fallen were almost drowned out by the sounds of battle. Almost, not quite.

At the center of the chaos, where the battle lines would soon come to a head, two figures stood out amongst the rest. Despite being dressed in fatigues, these men were not soldiers. They carried no weapons. Their movements did not display the same skill or precision as the fighters surrounding them.

One of the men was tall, dark skinned, and carried a large, bulky camera on his shoulder. The other was a shorter Caucasian man wielding a microphone in his hand. They were reporters, and one of them knew all too well, they should not be there.

A nearby explosion forced the men to dive for cover inside the remains of a derelict building. The area was once a small village. The remaining structures were now little more than rubble, huddled together for mutual protection. The men passed under the remains of an archway and crouched with their backs to some debris. They were plastered in dust. The man with the microphone had a small gash on his forehead. A trickle of blood ran down the side of his face, marking a trail through the sludge. But he didn't care. He was grinning like a child.

"Did you see that?" The man with the microphone shouted. "This is awesome!"

His companion shook his head in disbelief, wondering how he had allowed himself to be talked into such madness.

"See it?" he shouted again, fighting to be heard over the sounds of battle drawing ever closer.

"John, it's all I can do to keep from shitting myself," the cameraman yelled back. "Why the hell are we here?"

"We're reporters, Andrew!" John snapped. "It's what we do."

"There's no way I'm getting paid enough for this. We're going to get ourselves killed!"

"Quit complaining!" John grumbled. "Get the camera setup. This is exactly what we need. Don't you dare miss any of it."

"I'm more concerned with how long they're gonna miss us," Andrew said, as he pulled the camera off his shoulder and messed with the controls.

John examined his surroundings, looking for the most dramatic backdrop to deliver his report.

Andrew muttered under his breath as he finished fine-tuning his camera, "This is nuts!

Everyone warned me. Keep away from Hunt, they said. He's crazy, they said. Cares about nothing but the job. Always taking stupid chances. Did I listen? Of course not! So, here I am stuck in the middle of a war-zone, about to get blown to pieces, and am I running away like a sane person? No, I'm setting up a goddamn camera!"

"Are you ready yet," John snapped, suddenly turning back toward Andrew.

He closed the side panel on his camera and hoisted it back onto his shoulder. "Ok," he snapped back. "Camera, shoulder, we're rolling. Let's get this madness over with and get the hell out of here!"

John's focus was now the camera aimed at his face. He assumed a solemn expression as his mind raced to organize his thoughts. He registered Andrew's raised hand, three fingers extended. As the count reached one, John took a deep breath.

"This is John Hunt reporting from Syria. The ceasefire enforced by the UN just three weeks ago is officially over. As you can see and hear, the fighting has renewed with a vengeance.

The rebels are attempting to force a breakthrough less than a mile forward of our current position. We've broken away from our protective unit to provide you with these exclusive pictures from the heart of the battlefield."

Hunt lowered the microphone and assessed his surroundings. Meanwhile, Andrew brought the camera down off his shoulder, cradling it across his chest.

"Get some shots of the action and let's get back to the Jeep."

"Thank God," Andrew stated, fervently.

He positioned himself close to the wall, using as much of it for cover as possible, only allowing his shoulders and the camera to peek over the top. Panning left and right, he swept the camera across the expanse of devastation before them, his frown deepening with ever increasing concern. After a few minutes he lowered the camera, scanning the battlefield with the naked eye alone.

"John." His tone was loaded with concern. "Is it my imagination or are those tanks heading straight for us?"

John looked up sharply and rushed over next to Andrew at the wall. He peered into the distance for several moments before muttering under his breath, "Shit! We gotta go."

"About bloody time!"

Their Army Jeep was parked a hundred yards away, behind a small dune. Without further discussion the men ducked back through the archway and headed in that direction.

As the Jeep came into view relief washed over them. The noise of the battlefield made them oblivious to the high pitch whine overhead, a sound which gradually increased as they got closer. They were running fast, John just steps behind, as Andrew touched the door.

Sound, heat, and pressure, combined in one heart-stopping instant. In a flash, both men were engulfed in a raging fireball and tossed into the air like rag dolls. For a moment, John felt weightless, peaceful almost. Then, nothing.

Chapter 2

Death was never a concept Hunt had previously devoted much time or consideration to, until now. The darkness was absolute, enshrouding him like a grave, and although he had no sense of his own physical form, his consciousness was active and aware.

At first, there was nothing. No sound, smell, taste, or touch. There was only thought. With no way to determine the passage of time mere moments could have ticked idly by or entire years could have flown past unnoticed. Eventually, something did break through.

The sound was faint at first, so faint in fact that John initially attributed it to his imagination. But, it grew in volume and complexity until he could no longer dismiss its' presence simply as a fragment of a fevered mind.

As the sounds increased, the darkness appeared to recede almost as if the audible intrusion was driving it back. Gradually the physical world began to come back to him, or he to it. He would never be quite sure.

The sound was mechanical in nature, and as the light gradually coalesced into more recognizable patterns, Hunt was finally able to determine where he was. His tactile senses were returning, and they were eager to inform him that he was lying in bed, covered with crisp white sheets. Standing by the bed was a woman, a nurse judging by the uniform. She held a clipboard and was busy making notations on it as she studied the various monitors that surrounded him. These were the source of the mechanical sounds.

Unfortunately, as John's senses slowly returned so too did the pain. His entire body felt a searing rush of molten fire in a single wave, making him cry out involuntarily, startling the nurse. She turned toward him, a warm smile on her young, attractive face.

"Well hello there," she cooed. "You had us worried for a while."

"H – hurts," was all John managed, his voice cracking with the effort.

"I'm not surprised. You're lucky to be alive." Her voice was filled with warmth and concern, and as she spoke, she laid a delicate hand on his shoulder.

"Andrew? He's ok?"

"You just lie back and get some rest." The nurse neatly sidestepped the question. "You've still got a lot of healing to do."

As she replied, she reached up to the I.V. drip hanging by John's bed and adjusted some of the numbers on the electronic display. Almost immediately John could feel an unusual warmth spreading throughout his body.

"There. That should help with the pain," she said, but John never heard. He had already drifted back off into a deep and restful sleep.

Over the course of the next few days, John

drifted in and out of consciousness. With each visitation, he was able to maintain his grasp on reality a little longer as his strength gradually returned.

Only the one nurse ever tended to him. The same attractive, young lady who was with him when he first awoke. She was always ready with a warm smile, calming voice and a gentle, soothing hand.

From this point forward, John's recovery progressed with startling speed. His assortment of broken bones began to heal, and in a matter of only a few weeks he was able to leave his hospital room, albeit in a wheelchair, and experience the outside world for the first time in what felt like an eternity.

Assisted by the ever-present Jane, John made his way to the hospital gardens. She wheeled him over to the side of a long bench. She then locked his wheels and took a seat beside him.

Hunt closed his eyes and inhaled deeply. The sun-warmed air filled his lungs, and for the first time since his ordeal began he felt he had finally returned home.

His face was heavily swathed in bandages, and rather than feeling the warming midday sun against his skin he felt suffocated by the pervading heat that was trapped within its folds. That, however, was not the only thing that spoiled the occasion for John.

"You're thinking about Andrew again, aren't you?" Jane asked, softly. John's head dropped in a moment of defeat. "It wasn't your fault," she insisted.

"I wish I was as sure as you about that," John grunted sourly.

As grateful as John was of the companionship that Jane offered, he felt he didn't deserve it. He had spent the majority of his adult life breaking rules in his single-minded quest for success, all the while, heedless of the effects his actions may have had upon those around him. It was proving difficult, however, to ignore the harsh consequences of his latest escapade. The personal cost alone was challenging enough. His brutally ravaged face and numerous physical injuries all served as a constant reminder of both his selfishness and his abject stupidity. When all was said and done.

However, he was still alive. The knowledge that his actions had directly contributed to the death of his colleague, Andrew, was a crushing weight that threatened to suffocate him. All of his injuries paled into insignificance when compared with the guilt he now felt.

Jane knew there was nothing she could do to lift John's mood. She edged a little closer and rested a hand on his thigh in a show of companionship. After a short time, John rested his hand over the top of hers, and the two sat in silence, each lost in their own thoughts.

Chapter 3

Another month passed, during which time Hunt immersed himself in his physical therapy. He worked with grim determination, pushing himself to the very limit of his endurance. His efforts were not without reward, however. After only two weeks the wheelchair was no longer required. He still had pain, but he bore it stoically, considering the independence gained well worth the price. There was only one uncertainty left now. He still, had yet to see his face. Today that would change.

Hunt was nervous as he sat on the edge of the examination bed in the consultant's office.

To control his anxiety he focused his attention on the man seated before him. Dr. Mantle was no longer a young man. His receding, almost white hair and heavily lined face marked him as one who had served his time well in his chosen profession.

As Hunt watched, the Doctor appeared to make some adjustments to his written notes. When he was satisfied, he placed the folder on the table and turned to face his patient, a warm smile on his weathered face.

"Well, Mr. Hunt, how are you feeling today?" His voice, though gravelly with age, was still somehow gentle and soothing.

"Pretty good actually," Hunt answered, a wry smile on his face. "But I am starting to get a little tired of these surroundings."

"I can imagine." The doctor smiled broadly as he stood and made his way over to his patient. "Well, let's see what we can do about that, shall we?"

Dr. Mantle put on a pair of thin latex gloves, and using a pair of surgical scissors, he began to cut away at the bandages around Hunt's face. He was very gentle and precise in his actions. As John watched each single piece of bandage being laid on the table beside the examination bed, his nervousness increased. Finally, the last piece hit the table. The Doctor placed the scissors on top of the discarded dressing and leaned in closer to examine Hunt's face, his own expression giving very little away.

"How does it look, Doc?" John asked, his voice soft and with a slight tremor.

"Pretty good, actually," Dr. Mantle reassured him, drawing back slightly for a better look at the overall image. "There's still a lot of work left to do though."

"Show me," John demanded softly. The tremor had gone, replaced by a determined edge to his tone. The doctor pulled a wheeled stool over so he could sit in front of John. His face betrayed a little of the doubt he felt.

"It's healing Mr. Hunt, but I have to be honest. It doesn't look pretty. Like I said, there is still a lot of reconstructive surgery to do and..."

"Show me!" John demanded, more forcefully this time.

For a brief moment, their eyes locked and the doctor detected an edge of steel in John's demeanor. With a sigh of defeat, he turned away, reaching for a small handheld mirror, half buried under discarded dressings on the table. The doctor handed the mirror to John without a word and watched as he brought it to his face.

This was the first time John saw his face in almost six months. Despite his stern exterior, inside he was torn between anticipation and dread. He held the mirror rock steady before his face, while his free right hand slowly rose to his right cheek, gently brushing against the skin.

The degree of disfigurement was enormous. It looked as if someone had taken a blowtorch to the right side of his face and melted it away. His mouth and eyelid both drooped downward while the skin between them hung loosely. There was no structure to his cheek, merely a patchwork of crisscrossed scar tissue, red, swollen and angry. Finally, John pulled the mirror away without a word.

His mind was in turmoil. Wave after wave of intense emotions assaulted his consciousness. Grief, loss, despair, all clamored for attention only to be consumed by an overpowering rage. Hunt had dealt with so much over the past few months, but this was almost more than he could bear. It had taken every ounce of control that he possessed to stop him from throwing the mirror across the room in disgust. All traces of the man he knew were gone, replaced by something monstrous. Hunt swallowed hard, fighting the urge to weep.

"I'm sorry, Mr. Hunt," Dr. Mantle murmured, his tone full of sympathy. "We were lucky to save as much of your face as we did. The damage was extensive. Most of the bone structure had been crushed to a virtual powder. We rebuilt what we could with what was available, which wasn't much. Like I said, there is still a lot of work to do. Muscle and skin grafts, bone reconstruction…"

"Forget it, Doc," John interrupted, sharply, taking the doctor by surprise.

"Excuse me?"

Hunt's voice was flat, devoid of all emotion.

"I said forget it. There won't be any reconstruction."

"I realize this must be very distressing for you," the doctor stated, in a placating manner. "But I really don't think this is the right time to be making decisions of this magnitude."

A wry smile took over Hunt's face, oddly distorted by his disfigurement.

"Take a good look Doc. Do you believe I give a damn what you think? You did your job. Thanks. It's time for me to leave!"

"Look, Mr. Hunt, John." Dr. Mantle urged, using John's Christian name for the first time to breed some sort of camaraderie. "I can't let you leave. We need more time."

"Am I fit?" John asked.

"The progress you've made is astounding." Dr. Mantle answered, his voice tinged with admiration. "The Physical Therapist reports are encouraging and…"

"Am I fit?" John persisted.

The Doctor hesitated a moment. His dilemma was profound. If he answered truthfully, he would lose all control. Doing what was right for his patient, therefore, meant lying. He shook his head in frustration.

"Yes, Mr. Hunt," he confirmed, finally. "Technically you are."

"Then this conversation is over." John could see the pain this decision was causing the doctor and felt a momentary pang of guilt. "Don't think I'm not grateful, I am. But your work is done. If there is any healing left, it has to be done by me, back in the real world."

There was silence for a few moments as Dr. Mantle considered Hunt's words. He realized, however reluctantly, he had to admit defeat.

"This is against my better judgment,"

"So noted, Doc."

Chapter 4

Three hours and a mound of signed papers later, John finally found himself standing at the hospital's main entrance. The massive, glass-walled frontage stood like some transparent, mystical barrier between himself and the world outside.

Stoke-on-Trent, he thought, feeling warm about his home town. *Despite its faults it's good to be back in England.*

But as quickly as that warmth filled him, doubt rushed in, chilling him. He hesitated, unsure. For the past six months he had been isolated from the world and from the consequences of his actions. For the first time, his bravado was faltering.

As he stood indecisively at the threshold, he felt a light touch on his shoulder. It was familiar in its gentleness. He had felt it countless times over the past six months, and each time it brought him comfort and strength. He turned to face the softly smiling face of Jane, his nurse.

"Mr. Hunt," she said, in her soft, musical voice. "I wanted to catch you before you left."

Hunt was silent. He knew he should say something, but none of his usual sarcastic responses fit the moment.

"So, what are you going to do?" She asked gently.

Hunt shrugged. "I've got a life to rebuild I guess." He paused as doubt crept across his distorted features. "Six months. It's a long time. There's a lot to do."

Jane nodded, her face sympathetic. "Yes, I can imagine there is." Her gaze dropped.

Hunt's gaze followed, and for the first time, he noticed a small parcel in her hand. It was wrapped in brown paper and tied with brown string. She offered the package up to him.

"I thought this might help a little." A hint of nervousness in her voice.

"What is it?"

"Just a few news clippings and pictures I've been collecting these past months."

"Why?"

"I just thought they might be useful to you." She looked embarrassed. "Please, take it."

"I don't know what to say." He took the package from her, feeling strangely awkward as he did so. She smiled warmly at him.

"You could always try, thank you," she responded, in a mischievous tone.

John smiled. "I guess so." Their eyes locked together momentarily. "Thank you."

The moment was rudely interrupted by a high pitched beeping noise. Jane glanced down, pulled the pager off her belt, a look of irritation briefly crossing her face, then turned back to Hunt.

"Emergency. I have to go. Be careful Mr. Hunt."

John didn't get a chance to respond as she turned on her heel and strode off, full of purpose.

Hunt watched her back disappear around a corner before softly whispering his response.

"I will. Thank you."

As John turned toward the entrance, he realized that the thought of leaving the hospital no longer felt as daunting as it did only a few moments before. Shaking his head he exited through the double glass doors of the entrance and began the long trek home.

It was at least a couple of miles from the hospital to his home, and Hunt knew he should have taken a taxi. Although technically fit, he was still recovering, and the walk was really more grueling than he expected. But Hunt needed to feel fresh air again, needed to be surrounded by the hustle and bustle of people going about their daily lives, needed to consider a return to normality again. That was, he felt, worth the pain.

It was strange to be walking through his hometown again. Hunt was not typical of most journalists. He didn't like to be based in the hubs of journalistic action. His offices were in Birmingham, but rather than live there, John chose to commute from his place of birth, Stoke-on-Trent.

He had a small, two bedroom apartment in a high-rise just off the edge of the city, close to the University. There was a park nearby where he would take early morning walks and hit a few interesting watering holes frequented by students. He liked the atmosphere, he also liked the wealth of unattached females these places attracted. They were good places for feeding his ego, both physically and psychologically.

There was no sense of opulence in Hunt's apartment. It was comfortable in a utilitarian sort of way. Everything had its proper place.

Hunt entered, removed his coat and tossed it carelessly over the back of a deep leather armchair. He moved over to a drinks cabinet on the far wall, placing the parcel the nurse gave him onto his desk as he passed it.

When it came to drinks Hunt believed himself to be something of a connoisseur, preferring single malt whiskeys over anything else. He had a particular preference for Islay malts, and two brands, in particular, stood at the forefront of his collection, Lagavulin and

Bruichladdich. Today Hunt needed something with real bite. He pulled the cork on the Lagavulin and poured a generous measure into a tumbler, inhaling the rich, peaty aroma as he brought the glass up to his lips to savor the strong, smoky taste as he rolled the dark liquid around his mouth.

With tumbler in hand, Hunt turned and surveyed his living room. Two things immediately caught his attention. The first was the overflowing mail basket attached to the rear of the apartment door, just below the letterbox. A significant portion of the letters appeared to be in brown envelopes. That usually indicated official documents of either governmental or legal origin. He decided to ignore those for the moment, turning his attention instead to the winking light on the telephone answering machine that sat on his desk.

Taking another sip, Hunt walked over to his desk and took a seat in the swivel chair. He sorted rapidly through the thirty odd messages waiting for his attention. The majority were from well-wishers and so-called friends. They could wait.

One caught his eye. It had been left earlier that day and Hunt could tell by the caller I.D. that it originated from his offices. He pressed play and recognized the voice instantly. It was the cold, clinical tone of his boss, Alec Hartman.

"John. I hear they are letting you out today. It's about time. We need to talk. Call me, better yet, my office, tomorrow, twelve sharp. Oh, by the way, good to have you up and around again."

The machine clicked off. Hunt's face twisted into a bitter grin. "Nice Alec," he murmured sarcastically, staring at the ceiling. "That was almost sincere."

Hunt leaned back in the soft leather swivel chair, taking another sip of his drink, his face betraying a weary expression and muttered softly, "Welcome back to the real world John."

Chapter 5

The combination of single malt whisky and the pain medication Hunt was still taking should have ensured a peaceful nights' sleep. Unfortunately, this was not the case. A shaft of moonlight shone through the open curtains of Hunt's bedroom illuminating the bed, serving to highlight its disheveled nature. Amidst the mass of crumbled sheets lay Hunt bathed in sweat as he twisted and contorted in the throes of a nightmare.

Since first waking in the hospital several months ago Hunt's time and energy had been primarily focused on recovery. As a result, he had rarely thought about the events that had put him there in the first place. Now, back at home for the first time in several months, those events occupied his every moment. Every sound, sight, smell, and sensation came back to him in his dreams as vividly as if he were once again standing on the hot, unforgiving desert floor.

Those final moments, as he and Andrew ran towards their vehicle kept replaying in his mind. The acrid smoke obscuring their target from view, the drag of the sand on their feet, bogging them down with every step, and overhead, the high pitch whine of the mortar shell, it's steadily increasing volume signifying their doom.

No matter how Hunt replayed the events in his mind, the outcome was always the same.

He looked up at the vehicle. Andrew was about ten steps ahead of him and had already reached the jeep. He was opening its passenger side door. As he looked back at Hunt their eyes locked. At precisely that moment the mortar shell hit the Jeep, and Andrew instantly became nothing more than a brief silhouette against a fiery background before being utterly consumed.

The fireball expanded rapidly, reaching out towards Hunt.

"Nooooo!" Hunt screamed, sitting upright in his bed. The sweat running in tiny rivulets down his face, his breath coming in short, sharp gasps, rapidly steaming in front of him in the frigid air. His eyes wide open, panicked.

"Jesus John, You could wake the dead with a scream like that."

Startled, Hunt jumped backward against the headboard, eyes searching the room for the source of the voice.

In the far corner, by the window, he saw a figure. It was indistinct at first, standing at the very edge of the moonlight. But, as Hunt watched, it stumbled a few paces forward. As the figure stepped into the pale light, Hunt's breath stopped. The shock of recognition took him over completely.

"Lucky for you I was already awake."

The sardonic voice belonged to Andrew Johnson, Hunt's former cameraman. The figure standing at the foot of his bed, however, bore little resemblance to the man Hunt knew. The grinning face was mangled virtually beyond recognition. Bare bone protruded through patches of burnt and bloodied flesh. John's left eye was entirely white, cooked within the socket while the left side of his neck was wide open, tendons and bone clearly visible. The left arm was gone completely, only a mass of blood and bone remained at the shoulder, surrounded by heavily charred clothing.

During his many years as a war correspondent Hunt had witnessed some terrifying and gruesome events, but none of them could have prepared him for this.

"What's the matter, John?" Andrew asked as he began to shuffle around to the side of the bed. "Got nothing to say to your old mate?"

John tried to back away, bringing his knees up to his chest and curling up into a tight ball, burying his head in his arms. He started to rock back and forth, eyes closed, whispering softly to himself in a voice on the edge of madness.

"This isn't real. I'm still dreaming."

"Sorry to disappoint you, pal," Andrew stated. "But this is about as real as it gets."

"I'm hallucinating." Hunt insisted, continuing to rock, head down.

By now, Andrew's shuffling gait had brought him alongside Hunt. He reached out and laid his hand on Hunt's exposed arm.

"Does this feel like a hallucination John?" He asked softly.

John ceased rocking the instant Andrew's hand touched him. He brought his head up slowly, wide eyes staring in horror at the bloodied and blackened fingers resting lightly on his flesh. As John watched, Andrew calmly sat next to him on the bed. Suddenly, John jumped to his feet, his fear rapidly replaced by a panic-fueled anger.

"This can't be happening!" He almost screamed. "You...you're dead!"

"Aw, shit man. What gave me away?" Andrew laughed, the sound becoming a horrible wet gurgle inside his open throat. "Of course, I'm dead John Boy. You should know. After all, it was your stupidity and arrogance that got me killed."

"It wasn't my fault!"

"Easy John," Andrew said soothingly. "I'm not blaming you, merely stating the facts. You took us somewhere we had no business being. We were blown up. I was killed. Simple as that."

There was silence for a moment. Andrew watched John's face. It was evident Hunt was trying desperately to understand what was happening. It was also clear that he was failing miserably. This situation was so far beyond anything he had previously experienced; Hunt was having difficulty organizing his thoughts. The initial fear and shock of seeing Andrew, especially in such a grotesque manner, had rapidly subsided.

Hunt's first coherent thought was that he was mad. It would have come as no surprise had that been the case, but Hunt discarded the idea almost immediately. This wasn't madness, he felt sure of that, yet he still couldn't bring himself to believe that it was real. Dead bodies did not, in his experience, simply get up and walk and talk.

Hunt shook his head in defeat.

"I need a drink." He stated hoarsely, stalking around the bed toward the door on Andrew's side.

"Excellent idea John," Andrew responded pleasantly, rising from the bed. "I'll join you."

Hunt ignored Andrew as he stormed out of the bedroom. Andrew was only a few steps behind him when Hunt slammed the door closed.

"Cute John. Very cute." Andrew called petulantly through the closed door.

"What's your problem?" Hunt called back. "You're dead aren't you?"

Andrew calmly opened the bedroom door and walked through, following John into the living room.

"Yes John, I'm dead. I am not, however, a ghost."

"I must be losing my mind," John muttered under his breath as he reached the drinks cabinet.

"Not yet Johnny boy. But there's still time."

Hunt ignored the apparition. His attention focused on his drinks cabinet. He felt a deep need for the kind of relief only alcohol could bring. He poured himself a large shot of Lagavulin, the dark single malt releasing a powerful odor of smoky peat into the air. Leaving the bottle open he downed the shot in a single gulp and immediately poured a second. Only then did he turn back toward Andrew.

"You're dead!" He stated coldly. "I know, I was there!"

"That you were," Andrew agreed. "But let's be honest. You weren't exactly in a fit state to take notice of your surroundings."

"SHUT UP!"

Hunt turned away from Andrew. Everything about his manner declared that he was currently holding onto his sanity by only the most tenuous of threads. He seated himself in the large, leather backed armchair, muttering to himself all the while.

"Ignore it, John. You're dreaming. This is some crazy nightmare, and any minute you're going to wake up back in bed."

Unfortunately, the nightmare would not go away. Andrew seated himself on the sofa facing Hunt.

"I'm afraid not, John."

John turned his gaze away from his former cameraman, focusing instead on the contents of his glass. Andrew sighed.

"And ignoring me isn't going to help you."

Andrew leaned back comfortably and crossed his legs, a somewhat cumbersome exercise due to the mangled nature of his left leg. For a moment, the only sound between them was the steady drip of thick blood as it fell from the open wound where Andrew's left arm should have been. The blood hitting the leather arm of the sofa with a decidedly wet, sticky sound made John wince. It was Andrew who finally broke the silence.

"These past six months have been difficult for you John. I wonder, in all that time, have you ever asked yourself why you are still alive?"

John looked up sharply, his distorted features betraying both confusion and concern in equal measure. Andrew nodded.

"Yes. Interesting question, isn't it? I mean, you weren't much further from the explosion than I was. So how come I died and you didn't?"

A look of pure relief washed over Hunt, and for the first time, he actually managed to smile.

"Now I get it. This is some kind of elaborate hallucination. It's my mind processing all my bottled up guilt for what happened to you. Jane warned me about this, I just never expected it to be so vivid."

Andrew shook his head, "Is that what you seriously believe, John?" He glanced down at the dark sticky pool forming on the arm of the sofa. "Tell me then, would your mind go as far as to create a real bloodstain on your expensive leather?"

John allowed his gaze to fall on the arm of the sofa, his look of relief changing to one of incredulity. Slowly, he got up from the armchair, placed the tumbler on the table by its side, his hand trembling, and walked to the sofa. He dropped to one knee and dipped his index finger into the viscous fluid. Bringing it to his face, he reviled, his fingertip dark red, glistening. Andrew watched in silence, a slight, almost mocking smirk on his face. Finally, in a voice barely above a whisper, Hunt spoke, "This isn't possible."

"John. The fact that you are still alive is proof enough of the possibility of the impossible."

From the mantelpiece came the sonorous chime of an ornate brass clock as it struck the hour. Four o'clock. Andrew turned briefly at the sound. When he turned back to John his manner had become brusque, businesslike.

"Ok. John. Take a seat and listen carefully to what I have to say. I don't have a lot of time."

Hunt returned to his chair, his face a mixture of fear and confusion, his gaze fixed on his dark red stained fingertip.

"I don't understand. What's happening? Why are you here?"

"The more appropriate question, John, is why are you here?" John looked up sharply, but before he could answer Andrew plowed on. "Like I said, you shouldn't be. You should be dead, like me, but you're not. These things don't happen by chance. There is a reason, a purpose, a design behind events of this nature."

"What reason, what purpose?"

"I can't say. It's not my place."

"Then what can you say?" John demanded. "Why are you here?"

"To prepare you. Warn you, perhaps. You will find out in due course. Until then, all I can say is be careful what you believe."

"What I believe?" John asked, confused. "I don't believe in anything. You know that!"

"That's my point," Andrew stated flatly.

John felt the need for another drink. He rose from his chair, grabbed the glass from the table and strode to the drinks cabinet. Shaking his head, he poured another shot.

"None of this makes sense. You tell me I should be dead. Instead, I was saved, and a reason you can't *or just won't* tell me about. You say I should be careful of what I believe - which you know is nothing."

John turned, glass in hand, and his frustration vanished. The room was empty. The only indication Andrew was ever there, was the pool of blood, congealing on the arm of his sofa

Chapter 6

The remainder of the night passed without event, much to Hunt's relief. He didn't return to bed, choosing instead to sit and ponder the unusual experience. By morning, he had virtually convinced himself the whole disturbing occurrence had been nothing more than a result of his fevered imagination coupled with a residual guilt at the death of his cameraman. Of course, he was struggling to reconcile this theory with the now, nearly dry, blood stain on the arm of the sofa where Andrew's apparition sat. This was going to require a little more thought.

As the sun gradually rose over the city, Hunt began his preparations for the day. A large part of him didn't want to face reality. However, he decided he would pay a visit to his employer. It wasn't going to be pleasant, but after hearing the message on his answering machine, Hunt knew it was unavoidable.

Standing in front of his bathroom mirror, Hunt studied his reflection. He was virtually unrecognizable now, his strong, rugged features cruelly crushed and distorted. As he ran a hand over the damaged portion of his face he wondered, not for the first time, at the extreme turn of fate which allowed his eye to remain intact. A single, incongruous point of purity nestled amongst so much destruction.

He needed a shave. Ordinarily, Hunt preferred a small amount of stubble styled into a well-controlled goatee. Unfortunately, facial hair would no longer grow on his left side, and a one-sided goatee would really not do.

It was a brief moment of levity which did nothing to diminish the rage building within. Without realizing it, Hunt was holding onto the edges of the wash basin with such force, his knuckles had turned white with the effort. His shattered image stared back from within the silvered glass, mocking, taunting him. It spoke of an end to his former life. No more lavish parties filled with attractive girls clamoring for his attention. Hunt knew he would still be the center of attention wherever he went, but now for all the wrong reasons. As Hunt finally realized the true cost of his actions the rage became uncontainable. With a wild, animalistic scream, he reached out, grasped the mirror in both hands and ripped it free of its mountings, casting it aside with such force that it shattered against the far wall. As the last shards of glass tumbled to the ground, Hunt stormed from the bathroom in disgust.

The journey to Birmingham was just over an hour, but it proved enlightening for Hunt nonetheless. His appearance caused a certain amount of attention especially from his fellow commuters on the morning train. Reactions were varied. There were the mildly curious who stole surreptitious glances in his direction when they thought he wasn't looking. Then, of course, the openly hostile, predominantly teenage boys who ridiculed and passed vile comments about him between themselves, choosing a vocal volume, guaranteeing the entire carriage would be privy to their discourse. Hunt's initial instinct was to approach the teenagers, stand up to them, show them the error of their ways. But he didn't, he couldn't. With shame he realized, he was no different to them. Had their situations been reversed, he would have been just as quick to belittle and taunt. How could he condemn them for something he would have done himself?

There was an upside to this situation. Hunt's appearance disturbed people so much that, even on a morning commuter train packed tightly with travelers, he found himself alone on a seat. Not a single person felt comfortable enough to approach his personal space by taking the seat next to him. Hunt smiled inwardly at this. In all his years of traveling, this was the first time he had actually been comfortable on the journey to work. The smile was laced with bitterness, however. He had never felt as alone as he did now, surrounded by people. The open space around him was a demarcation line that spoke louder than any words. It was as if disfigurement could be somehow contagious and no-one wanted what he had.

Upon arrival at Birmingham New Street Station, it was only a short walk to the offices of his employer. They lay in the heart of the Colmore Business District on Colmore Row itself, a street replete with multi-story buildings of varying designs. There was an eclectic mix of both modern glass and old, solid brick construction. Hunt's offices lay in one of the more modern structures.

The offices themselves reflected the exterior façade, neat, ordered, clean with workstations separated by gleaming glass partitions. As Hunt entered the main outer office, he paused as his senses were suddenly assaulted by the discordant cacophony the room generated. An assortment of telephone ringtones, workstation monitors playing a variety of news clips, one-sided phone conversations and a host of shouted debates carried out across the entire room, all gave rise to a wall of sound which became almost physical in nature. Having been away from the office environment for so long, Hunt now found this assault on his senses almost painful. It took him a few moments to acclimatize himself.

Initially, Hunt's presence in the room went unnoticed. However, the noise level in the office dropped as he proceeded inside. He ignored the startled looks on his former colleagues as he strode through the center of the room towards the large, heavy looking door at the far end. Without pause, and without knocking, Hunt opened the door.

Alec Hartman was a tall man, broad shouldered and with an erect, military bearing. Strong, chiseled features and piercing brown eyes combined to give him an intimidating appearance. This was something he generally used to great effect, cowing his subordinates into submission. This was perhaps one of the biggest bones of contention between the two men as Hunt appeared immune to his aggressive demeanor, something which Hartman could not understand.

As Hunt entered the room, Hartman was busy at his personal computer. His eyes locked on the monitor, nothing about his manner suggested he had registered Hunt's intrusion.

Hunt knew this was not the case. It was a typical Hartman power play, yet another office game Hunt refused to play.

Hunt knew what was expected of him at this point. He should stand patiently and wait for his master to recognize him before proceeding further into the room. With barely a pause Hunt strode defiantly into the room and seated himself in the somewhat uncomfortable high-backed chair across the desk from Hartman.

Hartman's gaze never left the computer screen, but Hunt detected the merest flicker of annoyance as it passed across his face. Without looking up, Hartman broke the heavy silence, his voice low and gravely. "I have to say, I'm surprised to see you, John."

"Well, your phone message was pretty clear."

Hartman finally tore himself away from his computer screen, a dark, brooding frown on his face. "You look like crap," he stated bluntly.

Hunt shrugged. "Considering the circumstances, I think I'm doing pretty well."

"Perhaps," Hartman grudgingly conceded. "I almost wish you hadn't come."

"Oh?" Hunt watched, expression guarded, as

Alec reached into a drawer at the side of his desk. He withdrew a plain, white envelope from it.

"Then I could have put off giving you this," he replied coldly, as he tossed the envelope across the desk.

It landed squarely in front of Hunt who stared at it but made no move. "What is it?" he asked softly.

"Your severance papers," was the simple response. Hunt looked up in shock.

"You're firing me?"

"Fired. Past tense. The papers were dated four months ago. I gave you three months' notice, which means you haven't been an employee here for about a month now."

"You can't do this!"

"Can and have John," Hartman replied smoothly, with only the tiniest hint of satisfaction. "Can and have."

"I don't understand. Why?"

Hartman studied Hunt for a moment his expression quizzical at first. Then realization dawned. "You really don't get it do you, John?"

Hunt was about to respond, but Alec interrupted with a raised hand and a stern look.

"No Hunt, let me tell you what's been happening here these past few months while you've been gone." Hartman leaned forward, resting his elbows on the desk and clasping his hands tightly, his anger palpable. When he spoke next, his voice was soft, threatening. "Let's see. To begin with, we had the entire weight of the military land on us like the proverbial ton of bricks."

"Why?" Hunt asked softly.

"Why? Why?!" Hartman was incredulous, and it showed both in his voice and body language. "I don't believe you." Hartman brought himself back under control with some visible effort. "Ok, let me explain the consequences of your little stunt. You took Andrew about three miles forward of the designated safe zone without telling anyone. The fact you were found at all was nothing short of a miracle."

"How was I found?" Hunt asked.

"One of the unmanned reconnaissance drones happened to be flying over the region you were in at the exact moment your Jeep was destroyed. They picked up the explosion on camera, and some bright soldier had the sense to examine the images enough to recognize it for what it was. The information was passed up the line and eventually a rescue mission was mounted by the special forces units in the area."

"Eventually?"

"As I understand it, a rescue wasn't originally going to happen."

"So why did it?" Hunt asked. This was the first time anyone had spoken of his rescue since he had regained consciousness, and he realized he had a deep-seated need to know what had transpired.

"It appears the same industrious soldier who had provided the initial imagery had the foresight to maintain the drone coverage in the area. Based on the real-time imagery they managed to obtain they were able to determine one of you, at least, was still alive."

"So they sent a team to come and get us. I don't see the issue."

Alec shook his head in disgust, when he

spoke next, his tone was flat, devoid of emotion. "Three team members were killed in that operation."

Hunt slumped in his chair, the news deflating his typical arrogance.

"Shit."

"Precisely." Alec continued. "You, and by association, this company are being held responsible for their deaths."

"This is ridiculous," Hunt declared.

"Perhaps, but it's happening." "And you think by…"

"I've not finished!" Alec interrupted. "The team not only managed to bring you and what was left of Andrew out of there. They also recovered one surprisingly intact camera."

Hunt did not respond to this. He stared at Hartman, a quizzical look on his face. After a moment, Hartman continued in a flat monotone.

"One thing I always liked about Andrew was how he used his camera. Whenever it was with him, it was on. Did you know that John?"

"All the time?" Hunt asked, softly.

Alec nodded. There was a momentary silence as Alec gave Hunt time to digest the information.

"I didn't know that," Hunt admitted. His mind was racing as he ran through many potential scenarios. Hartman didn't give him time to reach a conclusion.

"Considering the circumstances it was incredible there was anything worth looking at. As it turns out, the footage was very illuminating."

"I can imagine," Hunt stated, his voice tinged with bitterness.

"Yes, it leaves no doubt who instigated your little escapade."

"You knew that already," Hunt stated, dismissively. "True."

"Then bury it!"

Alec snorted derisively. "A simple, elegant solution. Exactly what I expected from you, John. Yet, utterly impossible."

Hunt was totally confused.

Alec pressed on. "Don't ask me how, but that footage found its way into the hands of Andrew's family."

"Dear God!"

Alec nodded unsympathetically. "Trust me when I say the military response to this fiasco was nothing compared to their reaction. They came out with legal guns blazing, and you are their prime target. By the time they've finished with you, you may wish you had never survived."

"This is madness," Hunt retorted.

"Mad or not, it's happening. And we are responding the only way we can." A certain smugness crept into Hartman's voice.

Hunt shot Alec an angry stare as he realized how much his former employer was enjoying his discomfort. "By putting as much distance as possible between us. Well, thanks for the support!"

"You arrogant shit!" Hartman spat, sparing no venom. "I'm not going to pretend I'm sorry to see you go. Your crazy stunts have finally caught up with you. Frankly, I'm sick of covering your ass every time you throw the rulebook out of the window. This ends now! This shit storm you've created is too big for even me to clean up. You're on your own, pal."

"You love this, don't you?"

Hartman ignored the question as he relaxed into his chair, his steely gaze never leaving Hunt.

"You've got five minutes to clear your desk and get the hell out of here. Then I'm calling security."

"Don't do me any favors," Hunt grunted.

Hartman watched as Hunt left his chair and headed toward the door. As his hand reached the handle, Hunt turned back, his eyes afire with hatred,

"You really are a special kind of bastard."

Chapter 7

It was well outside of the peak period, so the train ride home was nowhere near as crowded as it had been earlier in the day. There were none of the insolent youths aboard this time either, which was just as well. Hunt's tolerance levels were virtually nonexistent now. If he had to face the same degree of abuse he had endured that morning, his response would be violent and final. As it was, however, the carriage he occupied had only three other people in it and none of them gave him a second glance, so he was afforded the comfort of an entire table seat to himself for the duration of his journey.

His mind kept replaying the conversation with Hartman over and over. At least he *now* knew how he survived, but that proved little comfort to him. Four people had lost their lives due to his actions. His usual arrogance and disdain for humanity could not stand under the weight of that responsibility. Four families were now grieving the loss of sons, husbands, fathers, and all because of his impetuous need to get the story. That was a heavy burden and one he felt in no way prepared to bear.

By the time Hunt disembarked from the train his anger had dissipated, being replaced by deep despair. For the first time in his life, he felt genuinely lost. It was a feeling that was alien to him, and as such, he found it to be both unwelcoming and a little frightening.

It was only a short walk through the University Quarter from the station back to his apartment. Under normal circumstances it would have been an enjoyable and leisurely stroll. He would take the time to eye up the female students some of whom he would know from his time drinking in the student bars, and there would almost always be brief and pleasurable encounters with friends along the way. Today, there was none of that. Hunt moved with purpose, head bowed, totally uncaring of his surroundings.

Closing his apartment door behind him, Hunt felt a welcome relief, as the discordant sounds of the world were finally muted to little more than a background hum. He leaned back against the closed door and closed his eyes for a moment, allowing a momentary peace to wash over him. When next his eyes opened his gaze was cold, hard and firmly fixed on his drinks cabinet.

Last night Hunt had required a drink with bite and taste, the better to reawaken his senses. Today his needs were entirely different. Now his interest was in volume. He wanted to drink and drink a good deal. He tossed his jacket over the back of the chair and reached for a less refined beverage.

Behind his primary whisky selection, which was always kept proudly on show, lay the second row of inferior, blended malts. These Hunt primarily used for less discerning visitors or as mixers for long drinks. It was for this row he now reached, withdrawing an unopened bottle of "Bells". Cracking open the screw top, he poured a single finger shot into a glass and downed it in one gulp, rapidly refilling the glass as the burning liquid began coursing through his system.

With the glass in one hand and the bottle in the other Hunt turned and surveyed his room, much as he had done the previous evening. Once again his eyes rested upon the assorted envelopes resting in the cage on the back of his door. It was a safe bet there were solicitors letters secreted somewhere among the stack. Hunt was in no mood for those just now.

His gaze continued on, sweeping the room until finally coming to rest on the parcel he had placed on his desk upon arriving home the previous evening. As his eyes fixed on the simplicity of the paper and string wrapped shape his mind cast briefly back to the moment he received it;

"I thought this might help a little."

"What is it?"

"Just a few bits and pieces. News clippings, pictures. I've been collecting them these past months."

"Why?"

"I just thought they might be useful to you."

The conversation was easy to recall as was the image of the young nurse, Jane. Instantly Hunt began to feel a gentle warmth spreading through his body, and just for once, it was a warmth which had absolutely no connection to alcohol.

No other course of action was suitable to the moment, so with a mild, non-committal shrug, Hunt crossed the room, bottle and glass still in tow. He took a seat in the plush swivel chair behind his desk, placed the bottle and glass aside, and reached over to the parcel, drawing it towards him. "Let's see what pearls of wisdom you've gathered for me shall we."

It took only a few moments for Hunt to remove the string and outer wrapping, which revealed a plain white box with a well-fitting lid, much like a small shoe box. Removing the cover Hunt saw that the box contained a collection of what appeared to be news clippings. As he skimmed through the paper collection, he realized that these were all news stories concerning himself and Andrew.

The clippings were collated in chronological order, with the oldest at the bottom of the pile. Skimming through the articles Hunt noticed a definite change in tone over time. They began expressing concern at the fate of two heroic reporters, then sadness over the death of Andrew, moving on to confusion over what exactly had happened until finally arriving at disgust at the irresponsibility of one reporter in particular. As he skimmed through them, Hunt once again grew angry. He was about to toss the whole collection across the room when he stopped. What appeared to be a full page spread had caught his eye. He separated it from the rest, opened it, and sighed.

Holding the article in one hand Hunt reached for his drink with the other. As he took a long slug from the glass, he failed to notice the tremor that was rapidly developing with both hands. The article was a detailed account of the funeral of his cameraman, Andrew. He couldn't help but read it. Every word on the page struck him like a knife blow, but he forced himself to continue reading. Finally, he reached the end. He laid the paper on the desk in front of himself and sat for a time staring off into space.

"Shit," He murmured. There was nothing more to add.

Chapter 8

That night's cool, dry air made Hunt thankful. His extended visit in the hospital had taken him through the worst of winter and spring. Now, in the midst of summer, the nights were shorter and warmer.

Hunt had spent a significant portion of the afternoon sitting and drinking, while his mind had wallowed in the contents of the newspaper article he had read. There was only so much self-pity he could endure before some sort of action was required. For Hunt, that meant walking. Movement always improved his disposition.

Donning a three-quarter length suede jacket, he left the apartment with all of its accusations behind and took to the streets. He had no particular destination in mind. For hours Hunt wandered the city. Inevitably his feet led to the only place that made any sense.

Hunt had worked with Andrew on and off for several years, and in all that time, he never realized his cameraman originally hailed from Stoke-on-Trent as well. It never came up. But reading that article made him realize that Andrew's family still lived in Burslem.

It had been several months since Andrew's funeral, but it had taken place in Hunt's hometown. Opened in 1879, the twenty-eight-acre site, known as Burslem Cemetery, was intended primarily as a recreational park, with only five and a half acres being given over for the purpose of burials. Nestled in the heart of the city, this lush, verdant landscape now played host to far more of the dead than it did the living. One could almost believe it was a community itself. Row upon row of gravestones stood like tiny dwellings, just one more estate among the many that adorned the city.

Wide thoroughfares crisscrossed the cemetery grounds providing access for both pedestrian and vehicular traffic. It was along one such road that Hunt now found himself. He was flanked on either side by large, looming trees. They stood firm, almost like sentries tasked with protecting the dead in their place of rest. Occasionally, a light gust of wind would sweep across their branches, causing them to rustle against one another. The overall effect gave rise to the somewhat fanciful notion that the trees themselves were communicating with one another. Whispered messages being passed back and forth, discussing what, none could say.

It would have been easy to become lost in a place like this, but Hunt walked with confidence, allowing instinct and intuition to guide him. It was as if, from the moment he left the apartment that afternoon, this had always been his destination.

The gravestone was elegant in its simplicity. Carved from a single oblong block of gray granite, it had a slightly curved upper edge that was rough and pitted. The front of the stone was polished smooth, with an outer border slightly darker than the rest of the face, and the wording was as simple as the stone itself. No excessive eulogies or abstracted poetic meanderings, simply a name and a date.

Andrew Johnson
1987 – 2016

There were signs the grave had been recently tended. Fresh flowers stood in a small vase centered in front of the stone. In retrospect, it was probably just as well Hunt had chosen to visit so late at night. A meeting with the deceased's family would almost certainly have gone badly.

As he stood, head bowed, there was so much Hunt wanted to say, so much that he felt needed to be said. In the end, however, as Hunt finally raised his head to face the damning words before him what came unbidden to his lips were perhaps the simplest and most honest of words he had ever uttered.

"I'm sorry."

"Touching John, very touching."

Hunt's heart skipped a beat, but other than that inward expression of surprise, he remained still. He knew the voice, there was an element of predictability regarding its presence here at this particular time.

"I thought you might turn up," Hunt stated calmly.

"Well, you seem to be taking my presence a little better than the last time we met," Andrew observed.

Hunt turned to face the apparition, a mirthless grin on his face.

"Well, after the day I've had, even you could be seen as an improvement."

Hunt began walking away from the grave site, and Andrew quickly fell into step alongside.

"Ah yes," Andrew nodded in apparent understanding. "Hartman busted your balls today didn't he?"

"You could say that," Hunt grunted, not entirely surprised that Andrew was already aware of this. In truth, it was tough to be surprised at anything when you were talking to what was essentially a zombie.

"I wish I could give you a hand on that front," Andrew said with sincerity. Hunt cast him a sidelong glance, his eyes filled with sudden mirth.

"I'm not sure you could spare it pal." He cautioned.

Andrew laughed loudly, although there was an odd wetness to the sound that made Hunt wince momentarily.

"It's good to see you're getting your sense of humor back John," Andrew chuckled. The smile on his face turned suddenly serious. "You're going to need that before this is all over."

"When what's all over Andrew?" John asked showing some signs of exasperation. "I'm still waiting for you to tell me just what the hell is going on!"

"Like I said to you before John. That's a question I can't answer."

"It's not your place?"

"Amazing!" Andrew turned to John, his face showing mock surprise. "You were actually listening. Good. You'll get your answers, John, eventually."

Hunt turned away, shaking his head in disgust at his former camera man's reticence.

"If you can't give me any answers, then what the hell are you doing here?"

"Think of me as a guide."

"Guide?" Hunt asked incredulously. "What do I need a guide for?"

"In case you hadn't noticed, John, your world has changed.

I'm here to help you make sense of those changes."

"Well, you're doing a bang-up job of it so far pal," Hunt said, his tone derisive.

"Be nice now John," Andrew responded, a slight smile on his face. "Anyway, we're here."

"What?" Hunt asked in some confusion.

Andrew had stopped walking and was staring straight ahead. Hunt turned to look towards whatever had captured his attention so entirely.

Looking around, Hunt realized with surprise that they had covered the entire length of the graveyard. Before him stood a massive set of black wrought iron gates. He looked around in bewilderment. Their conversation couldn't have taken long enough for them to cover so much ground, yet, here they were. He was about to ask

Andrew how this was possible when he noticed the intent and serious look on his companions' face. Hunt's brow furrowed in momentary concern.

"What's wrong?" He asked. Andrew motioned with his head, and Hunt turned once more in that direction. It was only then that he noticed something that he had previously overlooked.

On the far side of the road, directly across from the gate a long, jet black stretch limousine sat parked. Its' lights were off, so in the darkness it huddled, virtually invisible. Standing at its side, facing Hunt, was a tall man. He was dressed all in black and wore the black hat of a chauffeur. His black gloved hands were clasped in front of him, and he stared straight at Hunt. A momentary chill ran down Hunt's spine as he made eye contact. He couldn't have said why he felt the way he did, but there was something about this man and this car that felt wrong.

"What's going on Andrew?" Hunt probed, his voice soft, eyes never leaving the dark figure before him.

"This is where your journey really begins John," Andrew answered cryptically. Hunt turned sharply to look at Andrew.

"Where am I going?" He asked softly.

"I don't know."

"Are you coming with me?"

"I can't."

Suddenly Hunt felt a wave of trepidation sweep over him.

"And if I don't go?" Hunt asked, a strangely childlike quality to his voice.

Andrew turned to face his former colleague.

"That's a choice you don't get to make, John. You wanted to know what had happened to you, and why? This is the only way you will get those answers."

Hunt looked back toward the figure. The journalist in him came to the fore. Hunt had spent all his professional life searching for answers of one sort or another. Throughout his career, he had faced countless challenges, and as far as he was concerned, had bested them all. Could Hunt actually turn away from this one now? Instinctively he knew it would be the biggest challenge he had ever faced. Of course, if that were the case, then the story behind it would be of a corresponding magnitude.

As the thoughts ran through his head, the expression upon his face changed. Slowly at first, but then with increasing confidence, the fear was gradually washed away to be replaced by a look of steel. His eyes became hard and cold. Andrew watched as the change occurred, his own expression revealing a certain amount of approval.

"Ok," John stated firmly. "I'm ready." He was about to start walking when Andrew's voice stopped him.

"Remember John, this is a world you've never encountered before. The rules are going to be different then what you are used to, and nothing is going to be quite what it seems. Be vigilant. Be observant. Above all, be careful."

"Will I see you again?" Hunt asked.

Andrew shook his head. "That's going to be up to you John. From here on in, everything will be dictated by the choices you make. All, I can say is, I hope so."

"Fair enough." Without another word Hunt turned and began walking toward the dark figure and the long limousine.

Had someone told Hunt that he would be acting on the instructions of a dead man, he would have laughed out loud. The concept was utterly absurd. Yet, here he was, doing exactly that, and he didn't know why. The events of the past twenty-four hours had knocked him so far off balance his brain was having severe difficulty in keeping pace. Yet, as strange as these developments had been, there was some primal instinct deep inside that assured him, he was doing the right thing. As much as he didn't understand it, he took comfort from that assurance.

Andrew watched him as he left the confines of the graveyard. His face showed concern in no small measure. Hunt reached the car, and the chauffeur opened the rear door. As Hunt ducked inside the vehicle, Andrew turned away and muttered softly under his breath.

"Make the right choices John, for all our sakes."

Chapter 9

They traveled in silence. There was no method by which Hunt could determine the time, distance or direction. The rear windows of the limousine had been entirely blacked out, as was the glass partition between himself and the driver. The ride itself was the smoothest Hunt had ever experienced in any vehicle. There was not a single bump in the road that he could detect. They may as well have been gliding for all he knew. The whole experience was decidedly unsettling as if he were seated in a dark, silent tomb.

The driver himself had said nothing upon meeting Hunt. There had been no change in his stony expression as Hunt had climbed into the vehicle.

Left with so little external input to work with Hunt's mind retreated somewhat, choosing to review events up to this point in the hope that he could somehow piece together a pattern of some kind that may help him determine what was happening. This proved to be a pointless exercise. Events of the past forty-eight hours were so far outside of his normal experience that, try as he might, he could derive nothing of any use from a deeper examination.

Hunt felt that his life was no longer in his control. This in itself was not a pleasant thought. Unfortunately, it was also not alone. In giving life to this line of philosophical meandering, Hunt had inadvertently opened a door to much deeper and infinitely more disturbing questions. Foremost of these the question of whether his life had ever really been under his own control and if not his, then under whose control was it?

Just at the point where Hunt felt his own thoughts could lead him to the brink of insanity, he felt an almost imperceptible change in the movement of the vehicle.

A few moments later the limousine stopped. The door came open without ceremony, and eagerly Hunt made his exit. He looked around to try and get his bearings, but it was a futile exercise. There was nothing about the street that was familiar in any way. It was narrow and dark, devoid of street lighting. Buildings rose on either side, the smallest being four stories tall. The close confines of the tall, solid brick structures gave the street an almost claustrophobic feel, made worse by the lack of illumination.

The limousine had drawn alongside the only building in the street which had any external lighting, a fact for which Hunt was very thankful. It was a four-story structure, quite drab in outward appearance except for the somewhat garish sign that hung over a large entryway where two large wooden doors stood open. The red neon formed a single word, "Exodus".

The rhythmic bass tones from within proclaimed, louder than words, this was a nightclub, though the name was unknown, a fact he found intriguing, having been a patron of every club in his hometown at one point or another.

Hunt was unsure what was supposed to happen next. The entryway to the club captured his attention, the bright purple glow from its interior spilling out into the street and standing in stark contrast to the gloomy surroundings. What gave him pause, however, were the two large, well-built men flanking the doorway. Their cold, stern glares and extreme physical presence was intimidating. Hunt stood his ground under their withering gazes, a study in indecision.

A third man appeared in the doorway. He was short, thin and wiry, dressed in a plain but well fitted three piece suit of dark gray with an open shirt and no tie. Judging by his salt- and-pepper hair Hunt judged him to be in his mid-fifties. The man was unique compared to the other three men Hunt had so far encountered. He smiled warmly in Hunt's direction and appeared genuinely pleased to see him. Stepping through the doorway, he extended his hand in greeting.

"Mr. Hunt!," He exclaimed warmly. "It is so good to see you."

Hunt took the offered hand, wincing only slightly as it was shaken with a vigorous enthusiasm which, Hunt was sure, left his arm in danger of being torn out of its socket.

"Have we met?" Hunt asked in confusion.

The older man laughed.

"No, Mr. Hunt. We have not, though I have been looking forward to it for some time."

"Really?"

"Absolutely!" the old man declared. "I've been reading so much about you. You've made quite a splash in the papers these past months."

"I can imagine," Hunt grumbled. Having read some of the articles himself, he failed to understand what could have possibly engendered a reaction such as the one he was currently experiencing. The old man sensed Hunt's mood.

"I do apologize, Mr. Hunt." The old man showed contrition. "I would ask you to excuse my enthusiasm, I really have been looking forward to meeting you. Please…"

With a wave of his arm, the old man motioned toward the club. With reluctance, Hunt followed the man into the building.

Walking through the main entrance hallway, Hunt struggled to believe he was in the same building. The exterior gave the distinct impression of an establishment low on funds and even lower on taste, inside it spoke of something else entirely. Not a single penny had been spared on the décor.

The main hallway gave way to a large, open room with a wood paneled dance floor at the center. A long bar stood to one side, and the outer wall contained a series of private curved booths. The bar and booths were on a richly carpeted raised level that ringed the dance floor. Multi-colored mood lighting featured throughout the building providing an almost classic, retro feel to the interior. The music was loud and rhythmical, but not overpowering and there was a steady background buzz from the patrons, of which there was a surprising number.

As the old man led Hunt to one of the circular booths, he took the time to study some of the other guests. Judging by the quality of their dress they were all in the upper financial bracket of society. High-class suits and dresses featured everywhere, and more than a few of the ladies sported what looked to be expensive jewelry. There was something else about the patrons here that was so obvious that it actually took Hunt a few moments to notice it. They were all astonishingly attractive, men and women alike, tall, slim, well-built and groomed to perfection. Not the crowd Hunt was used to seeing. As this fact registered, Hunt's analytical talents kicked into overdrive. He remembered Andrew's parting words, back in the graveyard...

"...nothing is going to be quite what it seems. Be vigilant. Be observant. Above all, be careful."

It was time for Hunt, the man to take a back seat for a while, and for Hunt, the journalist to enter the game. He seated himself in the booth that was offered and waited as the old man made himself comfortable at the table.

"What is this place? And who are you?" Hunt asked bluntly, pleasantly surprised by the fact that he didn't have to shout to make himself heard. The old man smiled warmly.

"Why this is..." he swept his arm expansively around the room. "Club Exodus, and I am its proud owner and proprietor, Mr. Bera."

"I've never heard of this place," Hunt admitted.

"I would be surprised if you had. Club Exodus is a rather exclusive, members-only club. We do not advertise or promote ourselves in any way. Our clientele are hereby personal invitation only."

"Really?" Hunt glanced around the room before continuing. "You clearly have a preference for a particular type of patron. Why am I here?"

Before the cheerful Mr. Bera could answer a young woman appeared at the table. She was dressed in a short tight black skirt and a low cut white blouse, which revealed a significant amount of cleavage. Her dark hair was tied back in a long ponytail revealing a long, slender neck and slim, well- proportioned face. She carried a round tray upon which rested two glasses. One she placed before Mr. Bera while the second was for Hunt.

"Why, thank you, Julianna." Mr. Bera beamed.

The young girl inclined her head politely and smiled at the both of them, then left without saying a word. Mr. Bera watched her leave.

"Such a lovely creature," he said eventually, turning back to face Hunt.

Hunt picked up the glass tumbler that had been laid before him, a look of suspicion on his face. As he made eye contact with Mr. Bera the man beamed encouragingly at him. Hunt took a sip of the golden fluid in his glass. He recognized the drink instantly, and his face showed obvious surprise.

"Bruichladdich!"

"But of course Mr. Hunt," Mr. Bera exclaimed. "Only the best for our new friend."

Indeed it was the best. As Hunt raised the glass to his lips, savoring the exquisite and unique aroma, he reflected upon the fact that he had never before been inside any establishment that could afford to stock such a precious single malt. Exclusivity, it appeared, had its perks.

"You still haven't answered my question," Hunt responded bluntly. For the moment, he set aside the question of how this man appeared to know so much about him.

"Ah yes," Bera conceded, relaxing back into the plush leather seat. "Your observations of our clientele were really rather astute, and of course, correct. Under normal circumstances, a person such as yourself would not have been of interest to us, no offense intended."

"None taken," Hunt lied.

"As we both know, however, your circumstances have altered quite dramatically over the course of the past few months. Even though you're not aware of it, Mr. Hunt, you are quite unique now, and that makes you interesting."

"Unique? In what way?" Hunt pressed.

Bera smiled, but before he got an opportunity to answer the nightclub suddenly went dark and silent. Hunt looked around in alarm thinking perhaps something serious had happened, a fire or some other such emergency that had caused the sudden cessation of light and sound. The other patrons were not alarmed. Quite the opposite. An air of expectancy filled the room as those who had previously occupied the dance floor moved calmly to its outer edges, their eyes never leaving the center of the room. As Hunt watched the activity, Bera leaned across the table and softly spoke.

"We'll have plenty of time to discuss your merits, Mr. Hunt. For now, enjoy the show." He sat back, a secretive smile on his face.

A single shaft of light erupted from above the dance floor, creating a near solid beam to the floor at its center. At the same time, the silence was rudely shattered by the dramatic sounds of classical music. It was an arrangement of string and brass, taken from the fourth movement of Anton Bruckner's eighth symphony. A steady rhythm that built rapidly toward a natural crescendo.

As the music played, the excitement level within the room increased, all eyes turned toward the center of the dance floor where a hole gradually opened about eight feet in diameter, the radius of the single light increasing to match its dimensions.

There was some form of riser beneath the dance floor, and amidst smoke and light, a figure began to rise up through the opening. The woman stood erect with her head bowed.

As the smoke dissipated, Hunt was able to make out more details. She was small, slim, almost waif- like, her arms hanging loosely by her side. Dressed in a single piece of diaphanous silvery material which draped over her left shoulder and tied loosely at the waist, very little hid her slender figure. The material sparkled in the light and was completely open at the sides revealing vast expanses of pearly white flesh. Her vibrant red locks hung in loose swathes, flowing like rivers of fire across her shoulders and back.

As Hunt watched, entranced, he found that his breath had caught momentarily in his chest. Her mere presence had caused his blood to race and his pulse to quicken. She was exquisite in every way and every single eye in the room, male and female alike, were in awe of her.

The music had stopped, and for a moment there was absolute silence as the smoke gently swirled across the dance floor. It was a moment of pure magic. Then her head slowly rose, and everyone could see that the beauty of her form was perfectly complemented by the purity of her porcelain features and her intense sapphire blue eyes that sparkled with a life all their own.

Looking up appeared to have been the signal everyone was waiting for. The entire room reverberated once more to the sound of music. This was no dramatic orchestral piece, though. Now the music began with a simple, elegant, piano introduction, slow, melodic, atmospheric. Hunt recognized the opening notes as belonging to a classical piano waltz composed by Claude Debussy in the early nineteen hundreds: La Plus Que Lente -- The More Than Slow.

At the first keystroke, the entrancing female began to dance. Her movements were slow, graceful, sensuous and entirely erotic. The nature of her virtually transparent gown made each movement a revelation as every curve and contour of her perfect form was gradually revealed to the audience.

Hunt was no stranger to erotic dancers. In the past, he saw a variety of such females perform in a host of establishments What he witnessed now made everything else pale in significance. This was pure art performed to perfection. Each movement was carried out with such grace and precision that many of the onlookers were visibly moved to the point of tears.

"Exquisite isn't she?"

Hunt was momentarily startled by the abrupt intrusion. He was also more than a little annoyed at the fact that his attention had been so rudely torn away from the entrancing figure on the dance floor. He turned briefly to find Bera staring intently at him. As the music changed tempo once more, Hunt turned back to the vision of womanhood as she poured her soul onto the floor with each new interpretation of the piece.

"She is the main attraction," Bera continued. "We are fortunate to have her dance for us every night."

"Who is she?" Hunt breathed softly.

"Her name is Eve," Bera answered. "Would you like to meet her?"

The question caught Hunt off guard. He turned sharply to face Bera.

"I can see that you would," Bera intuited.

Indeed, thought Hunt. Who would not want to spend even a moment in the company of so perfect a creature? It was the stuff of dreams. No words were needed, the expression on Hunt's face told Bera everything he needed to know.

"Leave it to me, Mr. Hunt." He rose and exited the booth. Just as he was about to walk away, Bera paused as if a thought had just occurred to him. He turned back to Hunt. "You are my guest tonight, Mr. Hunt. Please take the time to enjoy everything this establishment has to offer. No charge."

"Thank you." Was all Hunt could manage to stammer as his attention was drawn once again to the impossible beauty on the dance floor.

Chapter 10

Eve continued to dance for only a few more minutes, ending in a climactic sequence of movements that left everyone breathless. The choreography of her routine was perfection itself, leaving her crouched in the exact center of the dance floor which immediately began to descend at the conclusion of her performance. There was a momentary silence while the audience collectively attempted to re-engage their brains. Eventually, a deafening applause accompanied Eves' descent into the deeper reaches of the club.

Once she had disappeared, the club members milled about in confusion. Hunt himself felt almost bereft without her presence in the room, and as he looked around, he could see that it was a feeling shared by many.

The standard club music began to play, and this acted as a signal to the patrons that they could return to their previous activities. And while they did return to their activities, there was a difference, and big one. Previously the dancing and drinking was restrained, sedate. No longer the case.

The dance floor filled quickly, and the moves practiced by all participants were wild, almost uncontrolled. The music too had changed. Where before it had been steady and rhythmical, now it was erratic, almost chaotic.

Hunt watched in fascination as the whole club environment changed before his eyes. It began gradually, a touch here, a stroke there, a stolen moment of passion as lips met and joined. As he watched the intensity of these encounters grew exponentially. It was almost as if Eves' dance had been a trigger that allowed the patrons to release all of their pent up sexual desires.

While Hunt was observing these exchanges, Julianna appeared at his booth with a fresh drink.

It was only then that he realized he was holding an empty glass, yet he could not remember drinking its contents. He looked up at her smiling face. She appeared unaffected by the apparent descent into debauchery taking place all around her. As she casually swapped the glasses at his table, Hunt took the opportunity to find out more about Club Exodus.

"How long have you worked here?" he asked.

"Oh, about three months now," she answered readily.

"And this is normal?"

She glanced around, her smile broadening as she turned back to him. "Of course," she replied. "What did you expect?"

Hunt couldn't think of a suitable answer. Julianna noted his confusion, and it obviously amused her. She sauntered away, laughing softly.

For the next hour, Hunt was witness to a variety of scenes, ranging from the mildly erotic to outright pornographic. He would never have classed himself as a prude, and he knew that places such as this existed, even within the confines of his hometown. He had even thought about visiting such establishments, but that had been little more than idle fantasizing. Now his fantasies were in the flesh, in every sense, and he didn't know what to make of it.

At the bar and on the dance floor patrons cavorted in various stages of undress, performing a variety of sexual acts upon one another. But that was positively mild when compared with what was happening in the booths around him. The music was gradually drowned out by the sound of frenzied sex being performed throughout the building.

Hunt was not the only observer. At least half of the patrons that night remained fully clothed. Apparently, voyeurism was as much a part of the environment as the act itself. Noticing this Hunt took some time to scan the faces of the watchers. It was only then that he noticed something that had previously escaped his attention.

Across the dance floor at the opposite end of the room was a plain, wooden door. There was a brass sign on it, but at this distance, Hunt could not make out the words. His attention had been drawn to it as he watched a man and a woman head in that direction. The door was flanked by two large men who could easily have been clones of the two forbidding figures that had stood at the club's entrance. As the man and woman approached, one of the door staff pulled open the door and waved them through, closing the door quickly behind them before resuming his original position at its side.

Hunt was pondering the import of this observation when Julianna appeared at his booth. This time, she had no replacement drink in hand.

"Mr. Hunt? Could you come with me please?" She asked politely.

"Where are we going?" Hunt asked as he exited the booth.

"Eve has requested your presence."

Hunt thought it was an odd way to phrase things, but the sudden quickening of his pulse encouraged him to put the thought aside, for now. He motioned for Julianna to lead the way and she proceeded, grinning that now familiar smile.

Julianna headed toward the far side of the bar, with Hunt following obediently behind. Along the way, he found himself having to sidestep several cavorting couples and even a few triples. One such couple playing naked at the bar proved a little harder to ignore than the rest. The woman sat astride a tall bar stool, legs splayed while her well-built partner stood between them, hands on her hips, sweating and grunting with his efforts. Despite the intensity of the moment, the woman still noticed Hunt's approach. As he was about to pass them by she reached out, and with unerring accuracy, placed her hand on his crotch. It was fair to say that despite, his outward display of disinterest, this area of Hunt's anatomy had reacted to the past hours' stimulus with typical male predictability. Upon realizing this, the woman's hand tightened on the area, and she smiled warmly at him.

"Do you want to join us?" She asked in a husky, breathless voice.

Hunt smiled politely, and with no small measure of discomfort, he gently disengaged her hand.

"Not tonight, thank you," he replied and carried on walking, quickening his pace slightly to catch up with Julianna.

As they rounded the bar, Julianna stopped at a single door. The brass plaque on it read: Private – Staff Only. Just as she reached for the handle, one of the security clones seemed to materialize out of nowhere to stand in her way.

"Patrons aren't allowed back here," He said in a deep, surly voice, his cold eyes never leaving Hunt. Julianna's smile never wavered.

"Mistress Eve has requested his presence, Carl," she stated sweetly. "You could always check with her if you like."

Hunt was sure that he detected a momentary look of fear pass across the big bruiser's face. It passed quickly, being replaced with the angry, surly expression Hunt was so used to seeing. The big man reluctantly moved aside.

Julianna pushed open the door and led the way into a long corridor. Hunt was about to follow when the bruiser, Carl, leaned in close to whisper in Hunt's ear.

"Take my advice Hunt. Leave while you still have the chance."

Hunt looked at the man carefully trying to decide if this was a genuine warning or some implied threat. There was nothing in Carl's face or general demeanor that indicated either possibility.

"This way Mr. Hunt," Julianna called sweetly from along the corridor.

The bruiser looked almost fearfully in Julianna's direction before turning back to Hunt.

"Don't say you weren't warned." he stated in a threatening tone, before moving away back into the shadows.

In some confusion Hunt turned and headed through the door and along the corridor, hurrying now to catch up with the young waitress leading the way.

Chapter 11

The corridor along which Hunt walked held numerous twists and turns, and try as he might, once they reached their destination Hunt had absolutely no idea where in the building they were.

In truth, Hunt's mind had been preoccupied during the walk. Twice now, he had received cryptic warnings, first from Andrew, and now from the intimidating doorman, Carl. Hunt wasn't sure what to make of it. He prided himself on his survival instincts. They had rarely let him down in the past, yet now, they were silent. So what danger was he facing that warranted such warnings?

He was still pondering this question as they reached the ornate, dark, wooden doorway at the end of the twisting corridor. Julianna knocked twice on the door, the sound was deep, heavy. She turned and walked away, smiling, leaving him to wait alone for a response.

The wait gave Hunt some time to study the extraordinary craftsmanship evident in the door itself. What looked to be an intricate, hand-carved relief covered the entire surface. It depicted a variety of figures and scenes, most involving some form of horned, demonic motif or exquisitely represented nude females, their bodies entwined in various acts of a decidedly sexual nature. The imagery was provocative, erotic and strangely disturbing. Hunt reached out a hand with the intent of tracing the carving of two young women, but at that moment, the door opened.

He saw no-one on the other side, and after a period of indecision, entered cautiously. He was a few steps into the room when he heard a soft thud from behind. Turning quickly he saw that the door had closed, apparently of its own volition as there was still no-one visible in the room. Hunt assumed there was some form of hidden mechanism that operated the door, some cleverly secreted sensors perhaps.

He walked toward the center of the large room, taking account of the furnishings, noting a distinct baroque feel to the overall décor. An ornate, high-backed sofa and matching chair stood in the middle of the room around a low, marble topped table. Black was the dominant color. The windowless walls, ceilings, and the majority of the furniture were all a rich, velvety black with pearl white as an accent color featuring predominantly on the central rug and the ornate coving which circled the room. The general effect was one of stark elegance. The room was lit by two seven foot tall lamps, each standing in opposing corners. The stands were ornate silver, the shades a sheer, silvery material from which transparent crystals hung, refracting a kaleidoscope of color around the room.

Hunt had just reached the table at the room's center when he felt a light touch upon his left shoulder. Turning sharply, he came face to face with a vision.

Eve stood before him, her delicate, ruby lips curled into a slight smile of amusement. She was almost a foot shorter than him, her head coming to just below his chin and she looked up at him with those twin, sparkling pools of sapphire blue. From that moment, he was lost, and she knew it. Her smile broadened slightly.

"Good evening Mr. Hunt," She whispered.

Hunt wanted to say something, anything, but he could not. Every sentence that formed in his mind was instantly discarded as unworthy. For a man who had, until now, made a living out of his ability to use, and at times misuse, the English language, to be rendered speechless in this fashion was an unusual and uncomfortable position to be in. Yet, here he was, gawping like some love sick school boy who is suddenly faced with his biggest fantasy crush. She understood, and without waiting for a response turned toward a long, black, high- backed chez-lounge that rested against one wall.

The instant her gaze left him, it felt like he was released from stasis. Hunt realized he had been holding his breath. He let this out now as slowly as he could, all the while watching her every movement.

"I've been looking forward to meeting you," Eve continued in her soft, silky voice.

Watching her walk away Hunt noted that she had not changed clothes since her earlier performance. That same gown was draped over her shoulder, falling like a shimmering, silver waterfall to the floor. As close as Hunt was to her now, the gown did even less to hide away the wealth of pure, pearly white flesh that formed the perfect contours of her body, yet still so much remained, tantalizingly, beyond his sight.

It took Hunt a moment to realize what she had said, so lost was he in the sheer pleasure of admiration. He closed his eyes for a moment to concentrate. It was easier to think if she wasn't directly in his field of vision, although he strongly suspected that she would be forever burnt into his mind.

"Why?" He asked finally when he could trust himself to speak.

"Why what?" She inquired with an innocence he knew to be feigned.

"Why have you been looking forward to meeting me?" He pressed. "How is it that you even know me?"

"You really don't understand, do you?" She sounded surprised, feigned or genuine, he could not be sure. "You are unique, John."

"You are the second person tonight to use that term. Why am I so unique?"

Eve looked Hunt full in the face, her eyes hardening, losing some of their child-like sparkle.

"You died John, then you came back. Didn't you know this?"

The look on Hunt's face made it clear that he was not aware. The blunt manner in which the information had been imparted made it even more impacting.

"No," Hunt answered, his voice a little hoarse.

Eve watched him with sympathy. Slowly she seated herself on the chez-lounge, leaning comfortably into the high backrest. She motioned to the space next to her.

"Please, John. Sit with me."

It was a simple request, one Hunt did not feel inclined to ignore. As he moved to take the place beside her, his mind replayed the last few moments of conversation. Something wasn't right, a nagging inconsistency that his mind struggled to grasp. It came to him as he took the offered seat and faced Eve.

"What is so unique about me dying and being brought back?" He questioned. "It's happened to countless people."

"True," Eve agreed, watching Hunt intently. "And in every such case, there was the chance this would happen." She could see Hunt's confusion deepening. "Let me explain. When a person dies, there is always the chance that, at the point of death, they may undergo a change. If that person is brought back, they can bring that change back with them."

"What kind of change?"

"Admittedly, we don't know," she confessed.

"This is crazy!"

"No, it's what makes you special, John."

"Has this happened before?"

"Only once," she explained, "and that was a very long time ago."

The conversation had drifted so far out of Hunt's depth itwas bewildering for him. The concept he was trying to grasp was massive and required a significant element of belief and faith, neither of which had previously taken a prominent place in his life.

Eve could see the difficulty Hunt had processing this new information. In a gesture born of concern she reached out and laid a hand on his thigh. Hunt reacted as though he had received a mild electric shock, jumping slightly and grasping her smooth hand in his own. Their eyes connected, and Hunt saw the concern and gentleness within this radiant orbs. Eve raised herself into an upright position, bringing them closer together in the process.

"How is it that a young woman, almost half my age, could possibly know all of this?" Hunt asked in a whisper.

By now their faces were barely an inch apart. Hunt could detect the rich, intoxicating scent of jasmine and feel the warmth of her breath on his face. Her hand had moved from his thigh up to his right shoulder, gently easing him backward, deeper into the chez-lounge.

"I think you'll find that I'm older than I look." She whispered.

By now Hunt was laid as far back as he could go and Eve was astride his waist. As she sat upright resting her entire body just above his crotch Andrew's words came unbidden to

Hunt's mind once more, *"...nothing is going to be quite what it seems."*

Eve reached down and untied the silken cord which held her robe in place. Untethered, a simple shrug was all it took to send the flimsy material cascading from her shoulder. In the face of that perfect nubile form, revealed in all its glory, Andrew's words evaporated from Hunt's mind as swiftly as smoke on a breeze.

Eve leaned forward bringing her face once more before Hunt's and as their lips met, his last coherent thought was that dreams, especially fantasies, really could come true.

Chapter 12

It was after one in the afternoon when Hunt finally awoke in his own bed. An entire fog bank had rolled across the forefront of his brain, effectively obscuring any meaningful recollections of the previous evening. He could remember kissing Eve. The remainder of the night, however, was a murky blur of fleeting images. The alcohol played its part, but Hunt knew there was more. It was Eve. The mere memory of her was capable of derailing all rational thought. Her scent, taste, image, just the thought of her was enough to set his pulse racing once more.

Rising from his bed, Hunt realized that he was still fully clothed, and he felt remarkably refreshed. He moved steadily into the kitchen to make himself a coffee while he considered the events of the last twenty-four hours.

Even to a cynic such as himself, it was difficult for Hunt to deny that his life had taken some radical twists since leaving the hospital. The appearance of Andrew, the Exodus, Eve, everything appeared to be designed to lead him in a particular direction, to what purpose, though, he could not say.

To date, the flow of actionable information in his direction had been little more than the barest trickle. If Mr. Bera and Eve were to be believed, then, at some point during the last six months, Hunt had died. If that were the case then surely his doctor would have told him?

Hunt had a lead to follow. It may have been only the barest of threads, but for a man with Hunt's skills, that may well be all he needed to unravel the entire weave.

When all was said and done, Hunt was a man of action, he did not like to be lead. Here was something he could take control of, so having reached a decision Hunt took his coffee into the main room and sat down at his office desk. It was time to start making some calls.

Three hours later Hunt found himself standing once more outside The Royal Stoke University Hospital. He was experiencing a certain ambivalence regarding his unexpected return. The majority of his memories were centered around pain and discomfort, as such the place did not feature highly on his "must visit" list. Hunt felt thankful that he had managed to secure an appointment with Dr. Mantle on such short notice.

It was another five-minute walk through the twisting maze of corridors before he reached Dr. Mantle's office. A young secretary was waiting in the reception area and saw Hunt approach. She smiled warmly as he reached her desk.

"Mr. Hunt?" she asked, obviously expecting him. Hunt nodded. "Please, go straight in." She motioned to a door to the left of her desk.

Dr. Mantle greeted Hunt with a firm handshake as he entered, motioning him to a seat next to his desk. Once they were both comfortably seated the doctor fixed Hunt with an intense look.

"So what can I do for you, Mr. Hunt?" He asked seriously. Hunt felt a little foolish, sitting across from Dr. Mantle. His fears felt trivial, child-like. The doctor watched Hunt patiently, noting the indecision etched into his face. The only way forward was to plunge right in. He took a deep breath.

"Did I die?" He asked with a soft intensity.

A brief flicker of surprise showed in Dr. Mantle's eyes. He leaned back, settling deeper into his office chair.

"What do you mean?" The doctor asked cautiously.

Hunt's frustration was evident. He wasn't sure himself exactly what he meant, but having started he felt the only option now was to plow on.

"Back when I had the accident, did I die?"

"Why do you ask?"

This was the question Hunt had feared. He had no answer. However, the fact Dr. Mantle had twice answered his question with a question of his own, told Hunt everything he needed to know. The doctor was hiding something, and he knew what it was.

"I did, didn't I?" Hunt pressed.

With a heavy sigh, the doctor relented.

"Yes, Mr. Hunt."

So it was true. Mr. Bera, Eve, they were right. But what did it mean? And how did they know? Hunt needed more information before he could begin to answer those questions.

"What happened?" Hunt asked bluntly.

"Are you really sure you want to know?" Dr. Mantle asked squirming slightly in his seat in obvious discomfort.

"I think I need to," Hunt replied.

"Very well," The Doctor conceded. "In truth, you died twice."

Hunt listened carefully as Dr. Mantle described the events surrounding his death. It was strange, hearing someone describing your own passing from the world in such a clinical fashion.

"Your injuries were incredibly severe." The doctor explained carefully. "The fact that you made it back to the military base camp at all was nothing short of miraculous. You died in that field. You were clinically dead for nearly two minutes before the corpsmen brought you back. Somehow, they stabilized you enough to transport you here. On your first night under my care, you went into cardiac arrest again. To be honest, I thought we'd lost you that second time."

"How long?" Hunt asked. He found himself morbidly fascinated with the tale of his own demise.

"Almost ten minutes," Dr. Mantle answered softly. "I was about to give up."

"Why didn't you tell me?"

"In retrospect, I probably should have," Dr. Mantle admitted. "But you recovered from the experience well, and in all truth, you had plenty to deal with. I didn't think it would benefit you to know any of this."

"I see."

"Why are you asking about this? Has something happened?"

There it was again. Another question Hunt could not answer. He ignored it.

"You said I recovered well." His brow furrowed quizzically. "Was there... is there anything different about me?"

"I'm not sure I understand."

"Medically speaking, was I changed in any way?" Hunt persisted.

"No," Dr. Mantle answered confidently. "Medically speaking, you are the same man now that you were before the accident, barring, of course, a few physical changes." He indicated the disfigurement with a wave of his hand. "Why? Do you feel different?"

Hunt rose from his chair, thrust his hands deep into his trouser pockets, looking down at Dr. Mantle with a somber expression.

"If you had asked me that question two days ago, the answer would have been no." He murmured. "Now, I'm not so sure. Thank you for your candor Dr. Mantle."

Hunt left the room before the doctor could respond. Though he moved with purposeful strides, his back was bowed, and his shoulders were slumped as though they bore the weight of the world.

Dr. Mantle watched him leave then sighed heavily. He was about to turn back to his desk when the side door opened. The door connected his office to its neighbor, although it was no doctor that stood, leaning nonchalantly against the frame, arms folded across her diminutive form. It was Jane, the lovely young nurse who had tended to Hunt during his recovery.

"Well, that was an interesting conversation," she stated bluntly.

"You heard it all then?" The doctor asked, letting out another long sigh.

"Oh yes," she confirmed.

"He's starting to put things together."

"Not yet," Jane stated thoughtfully. "But I think someone else is."

"You don't mean..." The doctor hadn't finished the question before Jane was nodding in the affirmative.

"Eve?" He concluded in a shocked voice.

"He was with her last night," Jane confirmed in an icy tone. The doctor let out an explosive breath then shook his head in wonder.

"She works fast." He observed.

"Hmm, hmm," was the sullen response.

"But, why tell him everything?"

"Oh, she wouldn't do that," Jane observed sourly. "You know the way she works. She'll tell him just enough to win his trust."

"Do you think it will be starting soon then?" Mantle asked, a twinge of trepidation in his voice.

"I think it's already started," Jane answered flatly.

"So what do we do?"

Jane gave him a cold, hard stare. "What do you think?" She snorted derisively.

The Doctor cast a lingering glance about the room, there was a fondness in his eyes, an almost wistful longing.

"It's a shame," he replied. "I was just starting to like this job.

"As was I," Jane cooed. "Unfortunately for both of us, it wasn't the job we were put here for."

Chapter 13

After leaving Dr. Mantle's office, Hunt wandered aimlessly through the hospital corridors for a while. He had chased down his lead and had gotten a result, but had no idea what it meant.

John Hunt had died, twice, if the good doctor was to be believed. Twelve minutes in total. Twelve minutes during which his body had lain cold and unmoving under some frantic doctor's ministrations, while the rest of him, that part of him that made John Hunt, who he was, was somewhere else. Where? That was the question.

He wasn't going to get any more answers here, that much was certain. Hunt had come here looking for confirmation, and he'd received it, anything else would be pure speculation, and far outside the expertise of the good Doctor Mantle. It was time to head elsewhere.

Hunt's next decision was made by his body, not his brain. In fact, it was his stomach that was leading the way. The vague earthquake noises coming from that region served as a reminder that he had eaten nothing since waking. He was starving. This was not a time for his usual expensive, high quality, fine dining choices. Right now, Hunt's desire was cheap, cheerful, and filling. Newcastle town center was a mere twenty-minute walk from his current location, and he knew he could find exactly what he was looking for there.

The afternoon was cooling rapidly, but was still pleasantly mild, and the walk was not overly exciting. A dual carriageway, the A34, led directly from the rear end of the hospital grounds into the heart of Newcastle. At this time of day, it was still choked with the tail end of the rush hour traffic. Hunt didn't mind the noise. However, the exhaust fumes were annoying. After the first five minutes, he could taste an oily, metallic film inside his mouth, but he endured stoically, knowing before long he would wash it away with a classic, tasteless fizzy pop.

As he made his way toward the town center, Hunt found himself considering his situation once more. Both Bera and Eve had called him unique. It was an odd and strangely disturbing choice of words. Why unique? Eve thought Hunt's near-death experience had somehow changed him. But, how? He felt no different than he did before. He realized he was relying on information given to him by people who, until twenty-four hours ago, he had never met. How did they know so much about him and why were they so interested? Hunt shook his head in total bemusement.

He set out from his apartment that afternoon determined to find an answer to a single question, and that he had done. Unfortunately answering that single question had resulted in the creation of a hundred more. He didn't consider this to be a very fair exchange, and it certainly was not the result he had hoped for.

Eventually, Hunt reached his destination. The fast food restaurant was located in the center of the pedestrian area, well away from the mass of vehicles that created a steady stream through the city. It was tacky in appearance, both outside and in. The majority of the furnishings were constructed from plastic made to look like wood, good enough perhaps to fool the eye of a child.

As Hunt walked up to the counter, he considered his choices, taking in all of the variety displayed in bright, colorful photographs on the overhead sales board. He knew from extensive experience, nothing he chose would look like the images presented to him in the sales pitch. He ultimately decided on a simple choice, two plain cheeseburgers chased down with some black, chemical, fizzy sludge with ice. He watched as the young serving girl walked away to get his order. She was a little sullen having failed to up-sell his order to the requisite "meal deal". While he waited, Hunt got his wallet out to pay.

Opening the bi-fold, brown leather wallet Hunt was surprised to see a white card drop to the floor. He picked it up and examined it. Plain white, just slightly larger than a standard business card, it was of exceptional quality. On the one side was an ornate depiction, in embossed gold leaf, of the letter E in a circle, while on the reverse was a message, handwritten in an elaborate, cursive script.

My car will pick you up tonight
at 10 pm.
Same place...
Don't be late.
-E

Hunt could feel his pulse quicken and his temperature rising as he read the message. He was so engrossed in examining the card that he hadn't noticed the return of the young serving girl with his order.

"Excuse me!" She said politely, but firmly.

"Oh, I'm sorry," Hunt retorted quickly, thrusting the card into his trouser pocket. He handed over a ten-pound note in exchange for his food.

"Keep the change." He said with sudden generosity.

Finding a seat near the window, facing the street, Hunt unwrapped the meaty parcels. All the while he was thinking of the card he had just found.

Eve wanted to see him again. The thought alone was enough to fill his entire being with excitement and indescribable pleasure. He closed his eyes and imagined another night alone with her: the feel of her exquisite form, the silky smooth texture of her skin, the intense sapphire blue of her eyes, the warm taste of her lips, it all rushed back in vivid detail.

There was something more. She had the answers he needed of that he was sure. The more he thought about it, the more he realized she had led him here. It was Eve who had first told him about his death. Doctor Mantle had only served to confirm that assertion. So how had she known? They had never met before, he was aware that much. And now, for the first time since meeting her, Hunt found her beauty had lost a little of its hypnotizing sparkle. There was a game being played here with Hunt at the center. He didn't know what the purpose of the game was, but Hunt now saw Eve was one of the key players.

Finishing his meal quickly, he checked his watch. It was seven o'clock. He had three hours. Hunt decided he would keep his appointment with the seductive and secretive Eve, but now he intended to join the game as a player, not merely a pawn. He rose quickly, his face set with determination. Setting off along the pedestrian walkway, Hunt went looking for a taxi to take him home. Time was short, and he had a lot of preparations to make.

Chapter 14

The journey home was quick and uneventful. Once there, Hunt's first course of action was to freshen up. A shower and change of clothes was a must. He was still dressed in the clothes he wore the previous evening.

All the while Hunt was sprucing himself up, he was thinking about the night ahead. He felt he needed to take control of events this time around, but at the same time, he knew how difficult that was going to be. Eve had an allure that had so far been one hundred percent successful in destroying all attempts at rational thought. Somehow Hunt had to find a defense against her charms. Also, with the realization that he was being played, came the instinctive awareness that the game itself was potentially very dangerous. Both Eve and Bera wanted something from him. Until he knew exactly what that was, he needed to move with extreme caution, lest he tip his hand too early.

Hunt chose more formal attire on this occasion. It felt appropriate while also making him feel more confident and in control. He wore a light gray, perfectly tailored three-piece suit, with a single breasted jacket, and freshly pressed, light pink shirt. Black patent leather slip-on shoes completed the ensemble. Electing to forego a tie, he chose instead to leave the top two buttons of his shirt undone in a more casual fashion.

As Hunt checked himself in a full-length mirror hanging to the right of his main apartment door, he realized that, for the past day, he had not given his disfigurement a second thought. As he thought about this fact, the reason became startlingly clear. Of all the feelings he had experienced the previous evening in Club Exodus, acceptance had been at the fore. Neither patron nor staff had given any indication there was anything unusual or wrong about Hunt's appearance.

It was such a simple thing, yet, at the time, it had passed unnoticed. The natural cynic in Hunt struggled to believe that there was no ulterior motive behind their actions. His faith in humanity simply could not stretch that far. The more he considered this development, however, the more he realized that perhaps he had an advantage. This, all too willing acceptance and inclusion, was a potential weakness, one he fully intended to exploit should the opportunity present itself.

Satisfied with his appearance, Hunt checked the time. It was eight-thirty; he had ample time to allow for a leisurely walk to the meeting point outside the cemetery. Grabbing a knee length, black woolen trench coat off a hook by the door, Hunt gave himself one last glance in the mirror, and with a smile born of new found confidence, left his apartment, locking the door behind him.

Hunt's chosen route this evening would take him through Hanley city center in the direction of one of the many country parks that were scattered throughout the district. It would be a straightforward journey, and he had given himself more than enough time to complete it without any undue exertion.

It was not long before Hunt began to get the uncomfortable feeling that something was wrong. He was entering the main center of Hanley, and he was sure that he was being followed. He crossed a main ring road by the location of the old bus station, checking all around him as he did so. He could see no one, but the feeling would not go away.

There were few people around at this time of night. It was that strange time between the shops closing and the local bars and nightclubs filling up with drunken revelers. In theory, it should be difficult for a person to remain hidden from view, yet whoever it was, was doing an expert job of staying out of his field of vision.

As Hunt entered the pedestrian area, he decided to change his route. Despite all of the changes Hanley had endured over the past twenty years, Hunt felt he still knew his way around the backstreets and alleyways pretty well. Well enough, at least, he hoped, to lose his pursuer.

The main walkway reached a fork ahead. Hunt had already decided to take the left branch, knowing that just around the corner would be exactly what he needed. He quickened his pace slightly, trying not to be too obvious about it. An old tobacconist stood just up ahead and before that a tight, dark alley leading off to the left. It was for that alley that Hunt now aimed his steps. Reaching it quickly, he checked behind him once more. This time, he was sure he had caught a fleeting glimpse of his elusive shadow.

That was all the encouragement Hunt needed. Turning down the alleyway, he broke into a run, his adrenaline levels rising steadily now. As he sprinted along, he kept checking behind him and in his haste, he had neglected to consider another feature of his chosen escape route.

Approximately a third of the way along, a side branch led off to the left from the alley, ending in a cul-de-sac. Hunt had given it no thought and now, as he ran, looking over his shoulder, he failed to notice the arm that suddenly flew out from that side alley. A big, meaty hand grabbed Hunt by the front of his coat, and aided by Hunt's own momentum, lifted him off the ground and swung him in a tight one-hundred-and-eighty-degree arc, slamming him backward into the alley wall.

The maneuver happened so fast that Hunt had no time to prepare himself for the resulting shock. With the breath completely knocked out of him he slumped to the ground, gasping, and crumpled into a ball on the stone cobbles.

Hunt tried to put a hand out to raise himself back up to a standing position, but a large, leather gloved hand grabbed him by the throat and lifted him with apparent ease, pinning him off the ground against the wall. He tried to grab the thick, muscular wrist and force the hand away, but it was useless. He was too stunned and out of breath to be able to initiate any form of useful resistance.

As he hung, suspended by this brutish appendage, gasping for air, Hunt tried to make out who his attackers were. His eyes watered, making it difficult to see clearly, but he got the impression of some hulking shapes in front of him. One of them moved in from the left.

"You were warned Hunt," the deep, gravelly voice was familiar. "I told you to leave while you had the chance, but you wouldn't listen."

In a moment of sudden clarity, Hunt realized who was speaking to him. It was the doorman, Carl.

"I don't understand," Hunt gasped, painfully still trying to draw breath. "What have I done?"

"It's not what you've done. It's what you're going to do." Carl answered cryptically.

"What?"

Carl moved in closer, bringing his face right up to Hunt's left ear. When he spoke next, it was a dark, dangerous whisper that only John heard.

"We've got a nice, comfortable life here Hunt, and it's been that way for a long time. I'm not going to take the chance that the choices you make are going to mess that up."

"What choices?" Hunt asked in confusion.

Hunt's vision was clearing now, and he could see there were five attackers including Carl. The one holding him against the wall had relaxed his grip slightly. It wasn't enough to allow Hunt to break free, but at least he could breathe a little easier. Carlstepped back again.

"Enough talk Hunt," he answered harshly. "I gave you a chance but you wouldn't listen."

Hunt fearfully watched as Carl proceeded to withdraw a long, straight blade from within the folds of his jacket. It had twin edges which glinted wickedly in the pale light that came into the alley, and its total length was a little more than a foot, easily enough for the job in hand. Carl's face clearly showed what he intended to do next. However, he never got the chance.

Without warning, Hunt heard a strangled grunt from the assailant holding him. The man's grip released and Hunt dropped, surprised, to one knee while the big bruiser collapsed like a felled tree, flailing futilely at his own neck.

Hunt had no time to ponder this development as, before he could move, he felt, rather than saw, a figure pass swiftly over his head, rebounding off the wall where he had been restrained. Before he could look up, Hunt heard three more grunts of pain swiftly followed by heavy thumps. By the time he could view his surroundings there was only one attacker left standing. Carl was in a fighting stance, his blade held low in his right hand, face firmly fixed on the figure facing him.

It was this figure that also drew Hunt's attention, it belonged to a female. She was crouched low in a wide fighting stance with most of her weight balanced on her right leg. Dressed in a figure-hugging, one-piece black cat- suit which zipped up the front, calf-length military style boots and black leather gloves she looked both incredibly sexy while at the same time being extremely dangerous. She held a small curved blade in her left hand which reminded Hunt of an eagle's talon. Hunt was transfixed. He knew this woman, he'd met her once before under very different circumstances. The jet black, waist-length hair, the strong, prominent cheekbones and aquiline nose. This was Jane, his nurse from the hospital.

Carl and Jane were facing each other with respectful wariness, both poised like coiled springs. Hunt held his breath in rapt fascination. In the end, it was Jane who moved first. She lunged forward, obviously hoping to catch Carl off guard, but he had been expecting this and immediately moved to parry with his own blade, only realizing too late that the entire move had been a subtle feint. At the last moment, Jane ducked to the side and spun on one foot, bringing her tiny blade in a wide arc towards Carl's now exposed side. With a speed that belied his bulk Carl altered his direction just enough to bring his blade around and block the strike, but now he was off balance, and he knew it.

A breathtaking flurry of strike and counter strikes erupted as Jane inexorably forced the larger, slower man back, their blades igniting sparks as they connected.

Carl cried out in pain, his blade slipping from nerveless fingers to clatter uselessly on the cobbled ground. Carl grabbed at his right forearm, and Hunt could see blood flowing freely to the ground from his hand. Realizing he had lost this battle Carl cast a last, hateful glance towards Hunt, before turning and fleeing. Jane followed him as far as the entrance to the side alley before stopping to watch him make his getaway.

Hunt sat in silence, his back against the wall of the alley as he watched Jane return, her movements now casual and relaxed. She reached the first of the four prone figures and placed two fingers to his neck, checking for any signs of life. Satisfied, she wiped her blade on his shirt and put it back in her scabbard, then moved quickly to the next figure. The silence in the alleyway was quickly becoming oppressive.

"Are they.......?" Hunt couldn't muster the word.

"Dead?" Jane finished. Hunt nodded.

Jane took a hard look at Hunt.

"They were here to kill you. This seemed like a better option to me."

John was no stranger to death. He had seen it in a variety of forms during his travels to the world's numerous war zones. This was, however, the first time he had encountered people intent on visiting that fate upon himself. He found that concept disturbing in a way difficult to put into words.

"But why does anyone want to kill me?" John demanded.

By now Jane had finished examining the bodies and had moved over to stand in front of

Hunt. She crouched down to face him, a look of sympathy on her delicate features.

"They are afraid of you John," she said.

"Afraid of me? But I'm nobody."

Jane shook her head.

"You're wrong John," she said. "Right now, you are, without a doubt, the single most important person on the face of the Earth."

"Why?" Hunt pleaded. "What happened to me?"

"I can't tell you that John. That's an answer you'll have to find out for yourself. What I can say is that because of what has happened you will soon be making choices that will impact every living being on the planet and that fact is making hoards of people very nervous. There are going to be some, like myself, who will do all we can to try and help you, but there will be others..." She flicked her head backward, indicating the bodies behind her. "Like these. They are not interested in waiting to see what choices you will make, so they are going to try and stop you."

"But.."

"John," she interrupted, laying a gentle hand upon his shoulder. "I can't tell you anything more. I've probably said too much already. Besides, you have an appointment to keep, don't you?"

In all the excitement Hunt had forgotten.

"The Exodus," he anxiously replied, glancing quickly at his watch. Nine-forty, he had twenty minutes.

"You need to make that appointment," Jane insisted. "Can you do that?"

"I think so," Hunt answered.

Jane nodded. "Then go. Now."

John rose quickly, wincing slightly thanks to the bruised ribs he had just received. He paused, looking over the carnage in the alley.

"What about these?" He asked.

Jane snorted. "Seriously, John. I can handle things here."

Their eyes locked for a moment. Jane smiled encouragingly at Hunt, and he drew strength from that.

"It's going to be okay John. I promise."

Hunt nodded, although somewhat doubtfully, and made haste out of the alley, escaping into the night, Jane watching his every step until he was gone.

Chapter 15

The remainder of Hunt's journey was a nervous one. He maintained a steady, albeit rapid pace and kept himself, as far as possible, in the light, in the hopes that this would discourage other prospective attackers that may be lurking around. Every dark alley and shadowed doorway became a potential source of danger, and Hunt gave them all as wide a berth as possible while keeping a wary eye out for any movement.

By the time he reached the graveyard, he was thoroughly exhausted. The adrenaline had left his system a long time ago, and now all he wanted was to rest. His transportation, however, had already arrived, the chauffeur standing to attention by the rear door in much the same fashion as the last time they met. Hunt checked his watch and saw that he had made it just on time.

Climbing into the car Hunt allowed himself to breathe a little easier, and by the time the vehicle was moving, Hunt hadrelaxed back into the plush leather seats. This was the first time since the attack that he had felt safe. It may have been an illusionary safety, but right now, Hunt would take what he could get.

With every passing moment, his world was just getting crazier and crazier. People were trying to kill him now. Hunt was starting to understand how those little steel balls felt inside the pinball machines of his youth, bouncing around aimlessly from one bizarre interaction to another. That's exactly how he was starting to feel after the last couple of days. He no longer had control over his life, and the world had morphed into some strange, disturbing shadow of itself.

As Hunt finally started to relax, his pulse slowing, breathing returning to normal, he realized if he was going to have any hope of surviving, he needed to take back control of his life if that was even possible.

He put little stock in the information Jane had given him. As much as she may have saved his life, the story she told was simply too fantastic for him take seriously, but if he chose to disbelieve her, then where did that leave him? He couldn't be any more lost and confused than he was at that moment, that much was certain.

Ultimately, nothing had really changed. When Hunt had set out from his apartment earlier that evening, he had done so with a specific objective in mind. Despite the events since then, that purpose had not changed. He still needed answers, and he still felt that the only person who could provide them was Eve. Having reached that conclusion, Hunt decided to put all other thoughts aside to use the remainder of the current journey to prepare himself for his encounter with Eve. He vowed, on this occasion, their encounter would play out in a very different manner than it had on the previous evening.

Upon arrival at The Exodus Hunt was greeted by Mr. Bera himself who opened the limousine door, a wide, effusive smile on his face. The smile slipped only slightly as he looked Hunt over.

"Are you all right Mr. Hunt?" He asked with genuine concern. Hunt glanced down at his clothing, realizing belatedly thathis trousers and outer coat, in particular, looked crumpled and had picked up some dirt spots as a result of his encounter in the alley. Thinking quickly, Hunt decided not to reveal the truth about the evening's events.

"I had a little accident on the way here," he said evasively. "I didn't have time to change."

"Well, as long as you're not hurt," Bera stated warmly.

"A few bruises is all," Hunt assured him. "I'll be fine."

"Excellent," Bera beamed. "I wouldn't want your evening to be spoiled by such a trivial thing."

Hunt's suspicious mind wondered briefly if Mr. Bera knew what had actually happened, but a look at the man's face convinced him this was not the case. There was no obvious deception to be found there.

As Hunt was led into the club interior, he noticed the two doormen from the previous evening were missing.

"What happened to your door staff?" He asked innocently Mr. Bera shrugged.

"They didn't turn in for work this evening. I haven't had time to replace them yet."

"I guess you get that a lot in this kind of business?"

"Not as much as you might think," Bera admitted. "Still, I'm sure they'll turn up."

Hunt was not so confident. It was too big a coincidence for staff to go missing from The Exodus on the very same night that he had been attacked. Hunt felt sure that Bera wouldn't be seeing those men again, unless of course, it was face down in a river somewhere. This did, however, cause him some mild concern. If they were part of the group that had attacked him, then it was highly likely they would have friends amongst the remainder of the staff. Hunt realized that he was going to have to be extremely careful here tonight.

Mr. Bera led him into the main room. Looking around Hunt recognized some of the patrons from the previous evening. It was early so everyone was still fully clothed. Some were dancing, alone or in pairs, while others sat at booths or congregated in groups around the building, talking and drinking. The atmosphere was as pleasant and amiable as Hunt remembered.

Hunt realized he was being led toward the bar, not toward the isolated booths as he had expected. Before he could say anything his host turned and smiled at him.

"Mistress Eve has requested you visit with her directly," he said with amusement.

"Oh?"

"Yes. I think you made quite an impression on her last night," the old man smirked. Hunt had the decency to look a little embarrassed, but Mr. Bera just laughed softly.

"Don't look so worried Mr. Hunt," he said amiably. "It is not often that a man attracts Eve's attentions so, completely. You should feel honored."

Hunt didn't know what to say to that. Should he feel honored? Under any other circumstances, the answer would probably have been a resounding, yes. At the moment, however, the overriding feeling he was experiencing was one of being manipulated.

By now they had skirted around the bar, arriving at the door which led to Eves' quarters. Mr. Bera held the door open and motioned him through.

"I think you know the way from here Mr. Hunt," he mused.

As he walked along the twisting corridor, Hunt began to steel himself. He could feel a certain excitement already beginning to build in anticipation. With considerable effort he concentrated on steadying his racing pulse, taking deep, relaxing breaths. He chided himself for his foolishness. It had been a long time since he had allowed a woman to affect him in such a profound way, and especially after so short a time.

Approaching along the corridor, he could see Eve standing in the doorway, silhouetted against the soft glow from within the room. She wore a long, flowing, sky blue gown, trimmed with silver. It hung loosely from her shoulders, leaving both arms exposed. Open at the front the material was joined at the waist by two small, ornate silver clasps spaced. about three inches apart.

She was smiling as he approached. Before any words could be spoken, she reached up with both arms around his neck, bringing his head down towards her. The kiss was long, lingering and passionate, and at that point, Hunt realized just how much he had underestimated this woman's powers of seduction, while at the same time, vastly overestimating his own powers of resistance.

The kiss broke, and Hunt was led by the hand towards the large black sofa. He seated himself at one end while Eve took the other. She lounged back in a relaxed fashion, bringing one leg up to stretch the length of the sofa allowing the dress to slip away, completely exposing her magnificent legs. At the sight of them, Hunt began to feel all control slipping away from him.

"So what shall we do tonight?" Eve teased.

"We could start by talking," Hunt responded quickly.

"Oh."

Hunt plunged on, ignoring the note of disappointment in Eve's tone.

"I need to know what's going on Eve. You told me last night that I'd changed, I was unique. I need to know what you meant by that."

Eve smiled gently, sitting up and moving across the sofa until she was seated next to Hunt. She laid a gentle hand on his shoulder, and he felt his skin quiver in pleasure at her delicate touch.

"John," she whispered softly, bringing her mouth so close to his ear that he could feel the warmth of her breath as she spoke. "You are looking for answers, and I promise you, those answers will come. But you must be patient. To everything, there is a time."

John was about to answer when the door opened, drawing both of their gazes.

The waitress, Julianna walked through carrying a tray of drinks. Eve smiled secretively as the young girl took her time bringing the drinks over to the little marble table before them. She placed the glasses on the table with great care and then turned to leave.

"Wait," Eve commanded, causing the waitress to stop dead in her tracks. "Come here

Julianna," she ordered her tone softening slightly.

Meekly, holding the tray before her almost like a shield, Julianna walked cautiously towards her mistress, her head bowed in submission. Hunt knew this to be a distraction tactic, but he was fascinated nonetheless. As Julianna came to stand before Eve, she reached up and plucked the tray from the girl's unresisting hands.

"You are such a pretty girl," Eve cooed. She turned to Hunt. "Don't you think so John?"

John looked up at Julianna's blushing face. He remembered her from the previous evening when she had delivered drinks to his booth. She wore the same outfit now as she had then. Some form of uniform he guessed. That being said, it fit her lush figure very well, and she was undeniably attractive.

"Yes," Hunt answered simply. Eves' brow furrowed momentarily.

"So clinical," she stated, rising from the sofa to stand at the girl's side. "I think we can do better than that." She continued softly, reaching out to stroke the girl's face. Julianna jumped slightly as Eve's long, slender fingers brushed the side of her cheek.

Eves' hand slowly traced the girl's jawline and down her neck. Juliannas' head tilted back in obvious pleasure, her breath coming in short gasps. Hunt was transfixed. Eve noticed the rapt look on his face and smiled wickedly.

"I think we have an audience, my sweet." She whispered softly into the girl's ear as her hand traced along the line of her collarbone and then down the open line of her blouse between her breasts. "Why don't we give your new admirer a show?"

As she said this, her hand had found the tiny buttons on the blouse, and she deftly flicked them open with her thumb and forefinger. Without waiting for an answer Eve then used her free hand to pull the girl's head in closer.

Hunt's excitement had been mounting steadily to the point where he was breathing almost as heavily as Julianna. At the point when the two girls brought their lips together, Hunt knew the evening was lost. He resigned himself to the fact that he would glean nothing of any use from this point forward. Whatever disappointment Hunt felt at that vanished the moment Juliannas' blouse hit the floor.

Chapter 16

Once again Hunt found himself waking after midday, back in his own bed with little idea of how he got there. He shook his head in frustration. *God, I've become a walking cliché.* Faced with two attractive, ultimately naked, women he had transformed into a pile of melted wax, happy and willing to be molded to their will. Admittedly, from what he could remember, the remainder of the evening had been exceptional, if a little exhausting, but that was beside the point. He had gone to The Exodus last night with a particular objective in mind, and in the fulfillment of that purpose he had utterly failed. Disgusted with himself, Hunt rose from his bed and made his way into the kitchen. He was in sore need of caffeine.

A few minutes later, and with a steaming cup of fresh, ground coffee in hand, Hunt entered the living room and made his way over to his office chair. He sat staring off into the distance, taking the occasional sip from his cup while his mind turned over the events of last night.

It was clear that he needed a different approach. As much as he hated to admit it, confronting Eve directly was never going to be an option. He was no match for her charms, and although the evenings he spent with her were undeniably enjoyable, he was not getting the information he so desperately needed.

If he couldn't get the information from Eve, that only left the club as a potential source, unfortunately, Hunt had no idea where it was. So far he had visited the club twice, and on both occasions, he was taken there in a way that ensured he could not see where it was located. As for his return home, those events were clouded in so much fog, making it impossible to remember a thing.

He flirted briefly with the idea of quizzing his neighbors, but that was an idea that died in its infancy. There was no sense of community spirit in his apartment block. Residents generally kept to themselves and rarely interacted with one another. Knocking on a neighbor's door would probably breach some obscure social convention he was unaware of.

The next potential source of information would have been security cameras. In the modern world of technology, it often seemed that "Big Brother" was indeed watching one's every move. Unfortunately "Big Brother" had not seen fit to extend his reach to Hunt's apartment block. The structure was privately run, and the owners had never considered the additional expense of installing such equipment worth their while. Even if this were not the case, Hunt would still have been reluctant to explore this avenue. To gain access to such footage, he would have had to answer questions and provide information he was not prepared to give.

He had no wish to involve any outside sources in this venture. If he was to locate the "Exodus", he was going to have to do it himself.

Booting up his laptop, Hunt decided to see if the club had some form of on-line presence, anything that might offer him an address of some sort. After an hour of surfing, he gave up in disgust. He had tried every keyword he could think of, to no avail. The club did not exist. He was getting frustrated, without the clubs location he wasn't sure how to get the information about himself that he so desperately needed.

Just then he heard the opening bars of Alice Coopers' "Poison" sounding from somewhere nearby. Recognizing it as the muffled ringtone from his mobile phone, he cocked his head to one side and tried to locate the source of the music. It was coming from his trench-coat which had been slung over the back of the sofa.

Hunt raced quickly across the room trying to reach the phone before it switched to the voicemail. He just made it. Looking at the display, he saw that it was Alec Hartman, Hunt's former boss. This was not someone

Hunt had any interest or desire to talk to so he thumbed the end call symbol.

He was just about to toss the phone on his desk in disgust when he stopped. For a moment he stood staring blankly at the phone held in his right hand. Something had just clicked in his head, the glimmer of an idea. As it began to coalesce Hunt's expression changed, a slow, sly smile spreading across his face.

Moving quickly back to his laptop, Hunt began a new round of surfing. This time, his searching was far more directed and infinitely more fruitful. Twenty minutes and one software download later Hunt felt he had exactly what he needed to solve his little conundrum.

It was a simple, elegant and decidedly underhand solution that was totally in-keeping with Hunt's personality. Of course, his solution necessitated a further visit to the club during its regular operating hours. Hunt didn't expect that to pose any particular problem, and sure enough, a quick search through his wallet revealed exactly what he had hoped for, another personal invite from the enticing Eve. He sat back in his office chair, folding his arms with a self-satisfied smirk on his face.

The next few hours were devoted to personal hygiene and preparation. He chose a pair of sand colored slacks with a white shirt and a well-fitting tweed jacket and black shoes.

The most important aspect of his preparation involved his mobile phone. The first task was to ensure that the GPS function was enabled then he went through the entire settings menu making sure that all non-essential functions were disabled or reduced to their lowest level to save battery function. He had left the phone charging for most of the afternoon so that, by the time he left the apartment it was on full power. In theory, that meant that the battery should last at least twenty-four hours between charges. Unfortunately, his phone was nearly two years old, and the battery was becoming less and less reliable. He hoped that it would last for what he had in mind. Once everything was ready, Hunt left the apartment to begin his magical mystery tour for the third night in a row.

Chapter 17

The journey to the graveyard was without incident on this occasion although Hunt's paranoia ensured that he took a circuitous route to make sure he was not followed. He expected Jane to be somewhere around again, but if she was out there, she was invisible. By the time Hunt reached the graveyard, he was convinced he was alone.

No-one was outside to greet him upon his arrival so he entered alone, noting as he did so that two new faces were flanking the entrance. Although they were obviously different people, they looked just as hulking, brooding and every bit as dangerous as their predecessors.

In truth Hunt was glad that he was alone at the moment, it made what he wanted to do a lot easier.

As he entered and scanned the main room he saw the usual numbers of early evening patrons, dancing, drinking and talking. One figure stood out amongst the crowd, Julianna, she was just returning to the bar having delivered a round of drinks to one of the booths. He moved quickly to intercept her. She looked up at his approach, a smile of genuine warmth on her face. There was no hint of embarrassment as a result of the previous evenings' entertainment.

"Good evening, Mr. Hunt," she cooed brightly. "It is good to see you again."

"Thank you, Julianna," he responded nervously. "Could you direct me to the men's room please?"

"Of course, it's on my way, please, just follow me."

She breezed away towards the dance floor. Hunt followed quickly in her wake.

The toilet facilities were located across from the dance floor, along a short corridor. As they approached the corridor, Hunt noticed the guarded door he had observed on his first night in the club. It was just to the right of the hall he was being led to, and it was guarded tonight as well. Nearing it, however, Hunt could read the brass plaque upon it. V.I.P Section - Members only. He laid a hand on Julianna's shoulder when she turned he motioned towards the doorway.

"What goes on in there?" he asked.

"Oh, that section is reserved for our exclusive members."

"And how do you get to become an exclusive member?" Hunt pressed.

"Oh, Mistress Eve chooses them herself," she replied, then moved closer, her body brushing against Hunt's chest. "I'm sure Mistress Eve will be choosing you before too long."

Hunt coughed a little uncomfortably at this sudden familiarity. He made a move to go around Julianna, but she laid a hand on his waist to stop him.

"Would you like some help?" she asked, seductively, her true meaning abundantly clear.

"I... I think I can manage, thank you," Hunt stammered.

Julianna looked momentarily disappointed, but then she smiled, drawing a hand across his waist and lightly brushing his groin area as she did so.

"Perhaps later then," she whispered.

Hunt watched as she walked away, rocking her hips from side to side in that incredibly alluring way that every woman knows from birth. Hunt sighed heavily as he watched her saunter out of his vision, realizing just how dangerous a place this was.

Once Julianna was gone, Hunt headed along the corridor and into the toilets. It was appointed in pretty much the same fashion as any other such facility he had frequented. There were four of everything, cubicles, urinals and sinks with mirrors above. About the only thing that set this apart from the rest was the amount of space. He was used to these places being very cramped; such was not the case here. It was not a great leap of imagination for Hunt to guess why this was so, knowing the nature of the establishment as he did.

Thankfully he was currently alone. Moving quickly, Hunt set about examining the area for a suitable hiding place where he could leave his mobile phone. The rubbish bin was the obvious choice, but there was just too much chance that it would be routinely emptied each night. Hunt discarded that option immediately.

Just then someone entered. One of the patrons. Hunt hurried over to one of the cubicles and entered closing and locking the door behind him. As he sat on the toilet bowl, waiting impatiently for the other man to finish his business, Hunt was staring at the ceiling, idly considering and discarding options. It took him a moment to realize exactly what it was he was looking at.

At first glance, the ceiling looked much like any other. Constructed from two-foot, square, white PVC tiles placed onto a square lattice, it was a standard suspended ceiling such as was used the world over. The type designed for easy access. So the tiles were not fixed in place.

The man outside had finished washing his hands, and Hunt could hear the door opening as he left. Quickly he stood on the toilet bowl and reached up. He was barely tall enough at a full stretch to pop the overhead tile out of its framework. He moved it back slightly to give himself room, then reached inside and carefully placed his phone onto one of the neighboring tiles. Replacing the tile without problems, he then climbed down from the toilet seat and left the men's room. The whole exercise had taken less than a minute.

The first stage of his plan was complete.

With the deed done Hunt decided to get a drink from the bar to settle his nerves. He was somewhat curious as to what the night would hold for him. Based on the events of the last two evenings he felt reasonably confident that he wouldn't be bored. It was strange however, that he hadn't seen the proprietor, Mr. Bera. He had the impression the man was a permanent fixture in the building, so his absence was unexpected.

Hunt did not have to wait long. Almost immediately upon his arrival at the bar, an attractive waitress approached with a drink in hand. She laid it before him with a disarming smile.

"Compliments of the house, Mr. Hunt," she declared. "Mistress Eve would like you to wait here. She will join you soon."

Hunt thanked the girl and took a sip of the fine single malt. He could not fault the hospitality here; although, he wondered how it was they could know exactly what he liked. It was becoming a disturbingly common theme.

Over the past few days, it appeared every person he met, alive or dead, knew more about him than he did.

Hunt's quiet reverie was interrupted by the approach of a group of women. There were five in total, all stunningly beautiful and all wearing very revealing clothing. They formed a tight ring around Hunt, who just sat motionless, studying them carefully. The one in front of him moved in close, laying a warm hand on his thigh, stroking gently back and forth along the muscle.

"Eve thought you might like some company, Mr. Hunt," she cooed. "Do you remember me?"

Hunt thought a moment, casting his mind back to the previous two nights. Eventually, he did recall her face. She was the woman who had propositioned him at the bar the first night. She smiled as she noted him blushing.

"You do remember, don't you?" Her tone was incredibly seductive.

Hunt was acutely aware of the other four women. They had closed the circle around him and were now gently caressing various parts of his body. It was clear where this was leading, and the thought was having the predicted reaction on Hunt. At the same time, however, he was unsure of himself. These women wanted him. Right here. Right now, at this bar. It was the stuff of fantasies, yet the reality made Hunt recoil.

"You didn't want to join me then." The woman pressed on, her hand reaching the top of his inner thigh and moving across slightly. "But you do now. Don't you?"

Hunt couldn't speak. Part of him wanted to just turn and run, but he was surrounded. Still, he turned on his stool, shocked to find that the other women had been gradually shedding their clothing. In fact, two of them were fully nude and had pressed on ahead, kissing and caressing each other with lustful abandon. As Hunt watched breathlessly, the other two women continued to strip while the woman who had spoken to him took the opportunity to lean toward him, nibbling gently at his neck.

Hunt was about to jump from his stool and make a quick exit when Eve appeared. The two women in front of him parted to allow her into the circle. Eve was also naked. "I see my girls have prepared you," she whispered sweetly, as she eased her nubile form between his parted, unresisting legs. She reached for his belt buckle and began slowly undoing it.

Hunt knew any resistance was futile. Cursing at his own weakness, he succumbed to the inevitable. He turned toward the woman who had been kissing his neck. Bringing her head up to his level he leaned in closer meeting her wet, eager lips with his own.

Chapter 18

It was ten o'clock the next morning when Hunt awoke. During the previous day's preparations, he had made a point of setting an alarm for this time, not wanting to lose half of the day to sleep as he had been prone to doing.

He roused himself quickly, almost eagerly, heading straight into the kitchen for his usual morning caffeine hit. With coffee in hand, he then began working on his laptop. It was time to see if his carefully laid plans had borne fruit. He whispered a silent prayer to whatever Gods may have been listening as he opened up the new software he had downloaded the previous day.

The plan had been very simple in both concept and execution, but there were still things that could, potentially, go wrong. His mobile phone had been set to emit a constant GPS signal. Assuming that the battery had not run down overnight and that there was nothing to interfere with the reception of that signal by overhead satellites then, in theory at least, the software he was now using should be able to pinpoint a real- time location for his phone. If everything worked, a few clicks of his mouse should reveal exactly where his phone was located, thereby providing the location of The Club Exodus.

"Yes!!" Hunt exclaimed.

It had worked. On the screen in front of him was a map overlay with a single red dot gleaming brightly. He zoomed in on the dot to determine the street address. It looked to be in the middle of an old industrial estate in the Trentham area. Hunt had never been there before. He hadn't even known it existed. He noted down the address on a pad by his laptop and then set about making a new set of preparations.

Hunt was determined to find some answers. His urgency was fueled in part by the events of the previous evenings. While he could not deny that he had experienced an incredible amount of pleasure and sexual gratification beyond most people's wildest dreams, he recognized that there was an escalation in progress that was disturbing.

Each night he had spent with the alluring Eve had involved greater levels of debauchery and lasciviousness on his part. While it was certainly true that Eve had been the instigator of these events, he had been a more than willing participator. After three consecutive nights of ever increasing levels of sexual depravity, it was clear to Hunt that some form of test was being conducted. Eve wanted something from him, but he had no idea what. Hunt was well outside of both his comfort zone and his base of knowledge and experience. He had grave concerns about what would happen should he fail one of Eves' tests. The only way he could see to avoid that was to get the answers he sought and get away, as quickly as possible. Now that he had a location he could do some personal reconnaissance without any distractions.

The dress code for the days' activities was to be casual, unobtrusive. Hunt felt he needed to be able to fade into the background. He chose black denims and thick-soled, heavy, black boots, a plain, grey, long-sleeved shirt and black, light- weight leather jacket. With the address in his trouser pocket, Hunt set off on his quest for answers.

It took almost half an hour to reach the location his computer had provided. The old industrial estate had once provided a home to a factory of some description. Several large buildings were spread out over the area, all behind a high chain-linked fence that was accessed by a large double gate. Everything about the place was old, from the tired-looking buildings with large cracked and smashed windows and broken doorways to the high fence rust covered and overgrown. Everything, that is, apart from the chain and large padlock securing the gate, these sparkled as new.

Hunt surveyed the area from across the street, where he stood under the shadow of a large tree. There didn't appear to be any form of security around, but then, there didn't need to be. The chain and padlock hung loosely from the center of the gate, taunting him. There was no way of climbing the tall fence, and he doubted he could find a way of removing the lock without being seen by some random passer-by. Having finally found the location, it was annoyingly beyond his reach.

As Hunt was considering his options, of which there were depressingly few, a vehicle drove up to the large double gates. It was a high-backed, long wheel-based, white transit van. There were no distinguishing features that Hunt could see. A man exited from the passenger side of the van. He wore fairly nondescript clothing consisting of blue jeans and a white t- shirt which showed off his superb upper body to good effect. As Hunt watched with interest, the man walked over to the gates, unlocked the padlock, unwound the chains and pushed the gates open. They swung on well-oiled hinges, yet one more piece of evidence that this entire complex was an exercise in elaborate deception. Before the gates had even come to rest the burly man had climbed back into the van, and it was moving through the opening. Hunt had expected the van to pause at the other side of the entrance to allow the man to close and lock the gates behind. To his surprise this did not happen. The van continued deeper into the compound leaving the entrance open behind it.

"Almost too easy," Hunt murmured.

He waited until the van was out of sight before he made his move. Checking both ways for signs of oncoming traffic, it was a quiet street, away from all the main traffic thoroughfares; Hunt sprinted across the road and continued on through the entrance and into the compound.

His journalistic instincts were in overdrive now and they were telling him that the van was a subject worthy of his investigation. Keeping as close to the buildings as possible, he moved quickly through the center avenue, the tall factory buildings rising on either side. As he approached the corner of each building, he would stop and cautiously poke his head around to check the side alley before continuing on.

It was at the second such alley that Hunt spied what he was looking for. The transit had stopped almost a third of the way along. By the time Hunt had reached the corner both the driver and passenger had exited the vehicle. The powerful passenger was busily operating a large electronic roller door on the side of the neighboring building. Hunt suspected that it led into some form of loading area. The driver, meanwhile, had opened the rear doors of the van and was currently manhandling some bulky object from the depths of its interior.

At this distance Hunt could not make out what it was, the darkness from the interior of the van made any such determination impossible. Once the object was close enough to the open rear doors, the driver jumped down to the ground and pulled it the rest of the way, stooping down to hoist it over his left shoulder.

Hunt gasped involuntarily as he recognized what the man was carrying. It was a person. At this distance there was no way to determine age, but as the sunlight gleamed off her waves of golden hair, the gender became unmistakable. She was unmoving, and Hunt was unsure if she were alive or dead. He noted that both wrists and ankles were bound, and a gag was around her mouth. As it was unusual for anyone to bind a corpse in this fashion, Hunt surmised that she was alive still.

It was obvious from the way these two men behaved that they felt themselves to be safe and secure in this area. Not once did they check their surroundings, a fact which was much in Hunt's favor.

Once the driver had the unconscious girl settled comfortably on his shoulder, he headed off towards the loading area where his companion waited. The two men casually entered the building.

Hunt waited a few moments, allowing them time to get out of sight. He had no idea what he had stumbled on to. It was certainly not what he had expected. While in all likelihood, it had nothing to do with his situation Hunt still felt compelled to find out more. There was a young girl in trouble, and for the moment at least, it looked like Hunt was the only person who could help her. He thought briefly about calling the police, but that was not possible. He had no phone, his mobile was still somewhere inside Club Exodus. He had no idea where the nearest public pay phone was. If the girl was going to get help, it would have to come from him.

With a deep breath, Hunt darted out from the corner of the building, keeping low and to whatever shadows offered themselves to him. Reaching the van he dropped immediately to the ground, keeping the large vehicle between himself and the loading area.

Looking under the van he could scan the loading area without being seen himself. The area was empty, but Hunt was just in time to see a door on the far wall closing slowly. That was obviously the route the two men had taken.

There was a certain urgency to Hunt's movements now. He didn't feel he could take the chance of letting the two men get too far ahead of him. Glancing around to make sure the coast was clear, Hunt lifted himself off the ground and sprinted around the rear of the van into the loading area, heading directly for the now closed door.

It would appear Hunt's luck was holding. The door was unlocked. There was no window, so he had no idea what might be waiting for him on the other side. Crouching low to one side of the door, he reached up and turned the handle, cracking the door open a fraction. He fully expected one of the men to come crashing through from the other side, but nothing happened. Opening the door wider, Hunt poked his head through.

He found himself looking down a small, dark corridor which ended in a set of double doors. They were wide open and led into a large, spacious room. Moving cautiously once more, Hunt edged along the wall of the corridor in a low crouch until he reached the double doors.

He paused for a moment, staring ahead in confusion. Even in the near dark, this spacious room was familiar to Hunt. It was the main floor area of the Club Exodus. Hunt could just make out the bar and dance floor ahead, the booths to his left, and there, on his right, was the door to the VIP area. It was through this door that the men carried the young girl.

The situation was getting more bizarre by the second.

What the hell kind of place was Club Exodus? Hunt had come here originally hoping to find answers, but now, it looked like he was going to be asking a whole range of new and more dangerous questions. The club was in darkness, but there was enough ambient daylight streaming through the open fire doors for Hunt to see his way across the dance floor without mishap. Reaching the door to the VIP section Hunt paused, putting his back against the wall. The tension was mounting, his blood was racing. A large part of him just wanted to get the hell out of there. Every part of his brain was screaming at him to get out while he still could. Every part that is, except for the part that contained the image of the young girl slumped over the driver's shoulder. In the end, it was that image which spurred him on.

As the image gave Hunt renewed courage, he grasped the door handle and cracked the door open just enough to see beyond. It was a long, dark corridor, currently empty. With no further thought for his own safety, Hunt opened the door and entered, moving along the corridor with swift, confident strides.

It led into a large, circular room, with five other corridors leading off it, each spaced equidistant from one another. The room was empty and dimly lit from a single large candle burning brightly in a sconce on the wall opposite him. Hunt considered it to be an odd lighting feature in a place such as this, and he walked over to examine it more carefully.

The candle itself was as strange as its presence. Hunt could see the flame bouncing on the top of the wick, yet the wick itself showed no signs of charring, the wax remained solid, unaffected by the flame. Hunt brought his hand up to the flame and was astonished to find that it burned with no heat whatsoever. How was this possible? What did it mean? Hunt was so engrossed in his examination of the miraculous candle that he did not hear the two men exiting a corridor behind him.

The men had noticed Hunt immediately upon entering the room and had split up slightly to approach him from different directions. They moved with surprising stealth for such large individuals, and Hunt did not register their approach until they were a mere step behind him. He started to turn to face them, but the action was never completed. The large man in the white t-shirt pulled a set of brass knuckles from a trouser pocket and placed them over his right hand. As Hunt began his turn, the man launched a devastating blow to the side of his head that sent Hunt spinning to the ground.

As Hunt lay there, fighting to remain conscious, he just made out the images of the two men as his assailant turned to his companion and spoke.

"I think we'd better call Mr. Bera."

Hunt lost his battle at that point, and his conscious mind slipped away into darkness.

Chapter 19

The floor was cold and hard. Hunt groaned and rolled over onto his back. His head felt like it had been trapped in a vice, and the top of his jawline on the left side felt like it was on fire. He brought his hand up to the source of his pain, wincing slightly as his fingers lightly brushed against the swelling that had formed there. Opening his eyes slowly, Hunt raised himself up on his hands and shuffled backward until his back could rest against the wall.

The room was small and unlit, the only source of illumination coming from under the door in front of him. By its size, Hunt guessed he was being held in some kind of storage room. It had been emptied of everything, obviously so that there would be nothing Hunt could potentially use to facilitate some form of escape. It was odd then that he was not in any kind of restraints. Was he deemed to be so minor a threat? Hunt found that to be vaguely insulting.

He had no idea how long he had been unconscious; a few hours at least he would guess judging by the continual throbbing inside his skull. That was no mere tap he had received. As he thought about it, he considered himself to be fortunate that he regained consciousness at all.

Then his thoughts turned towards the girl. Remembering her limp form draped carelessly over the drivers' shoulder, he felt afraid for her. Anything could have happened by now. Was she even still alive? He couldn't just sit there, bemoaning his own fate.

Hunt was about to stand when he noticed a shadow under the door ahead, quickly followed by the sound of metal scraping against metal. He relaxed back as the door opened on silent hinges.

At first, Hunt couldn't recognize the silhouette framed in the doorway. The man entered, and he realized it was Mr. Bera. He was quickly followed by two hulking brutes. As Bera approached, Hunt noticed that his expression was one of almost profound sorrow. He thought it an odd emotion to be displaying under the circumstances. Reaching Hunt, the old man crouched down before him and smiled warmly. The two guards remained just inside the doorway.

"Mr. Hunt," he remarked, amiably. "You are awake. Good. For a time there we thought you might have been killed."

"So what happens now?" Hunt asked, sullenly.

"Now? We talk for a moment," Bera said, simply, his face hardening. "Mr. Hunt, how did you find us?"

Hunt considered the question for a moment before deciding that deception or obfuscation of any kind would serve no useful purpose.

"My mobile," he said. "I left it here, hidden in the toilets, then tracked its location this morning with GPS."

"Ingenious!" Bera exclaimed, appearing genuinely impressed. "You are such a resourceful fellow, Mr. Hunt. In my world, that makes you dangerous." His voice changed, becoming dark and threatening. "If I had my way, Mr. Hunt, you would be dead. Fortunately for you, that is not my choice to make."

"Eve?" Hunt surmised.

"Indeed," Bera confirmed sourly. "She is still of the opinion that you can be useful. For the record, I disagree. We shall find out soon who is right. I'm going to ask you to accompany my friends now. Be warned, they have explicit instructions to kill you, should you try anything."

He turned to leave, pausing as he drew level with the two guards. He looked toward the guard on the left.

"Bring him," he said flatly.

As he stared at the two huge figures standing mute in the doorway, Hunt knew he should be afraid. But he was not. Confused? Yes. Frustrated? More than a little, but afraid? No. He had no idea what he had stumbled upon here, some form of human trafficking he surmised. He had heard of such things, but had never thought they could exist in his own hometown.

The guard on the left motioned for Hunt to stand. He did without hesitation. He did not consider himself to be in any way heroic or courageous. He had some fighting skills, it was true. A collection of martial arts training in his youth with additional training added over the years during research for various stories all meant that, under normal conditions, he could handle himself pretty well. Here, however, he was under no illusions, either one of the two guards could break him in half with a mere look should they feel so inclined. As much as he had died twice and returned already, Hunt felt no desire to test his luck for a third time. For the moment, at least, he intended to follow every instruction, to the letter.

He rose quickly, experiencing a momentary bout of dizziness in the process. This caused him to close his eyes briefly to give his head time to settle. He was surprised but grateful that the guards made no attempt to hurry him along.

The guards led him out of the darkened storage area into a well-lit corridor, the sudden change in light level causing him to wince slightly as his eyes adjusted. The corridor was not long, and it was only a short time later that

Hunt and his brutish companions reached the point where it opened out into a room that Hunt recognized. It was the large, circular room where he had been accosted. He raised his hand involuntarily towards his swollen face as he remembered the blow that had struck him down so effectively.

An ornate chandelier hung from the center, overhead. Apart from the increased light level, the room itself looked no different. The large candle which had so captured his attention earlier was now to his left.

The guards led him to the center of the room and then stopped.

"Wait here," the guard on the left ordered in a gruff voice.

Hunt did as he was commanded, watching as the two men moved across the room to take up positions on either side of the candle. Aside from his own nervous breathing the room was still.

"Good evening, John."

Hunt spun around to find Eve standing directly behind him. He had not heard her approach, yet, there she was, less than two feet away. Oddly, she wore a plain white robe covering her form completely, her arms folded across her chest so that her hands were hidden in its voluminous sleeves. She had a smile on her face, yet her sapphire eyes appeared to burn with a cold fire. Before Hunt could say a word she took a step closer.

"I have to say, this is not the way I hoped tonight would go." Her voice was as liquid smooth as it always was, but now it held a hint of danger, a hardness that Hunt had not heard before.

"I'm not sure what you want me to say," Hunt retorted, his voice guarded.

Eve began to walk a slow, tight circle around him, forcing him to continually turn to maintain eye contact. In the background, people were exiting from all five of the corridors feeding into the circular room. They were dressed the same as Eve. There had to be at least twenty in total. A couple of faces he recognized as patrons of Club Exodus.

"For the moment, John," Eve responded slowly. "It would be wise if you said nothing."

The new arrivals spread out, forming a large circle around the circumference of the room.

Each of them stood with arms crossed into their sleeves and heads bowed.

"The past three nights have been a test. You must have realized that."

"It had crossed my mind," Hunt admitted. He wanted to say more but restrained himself, figuring it was probably better to let Eve reveal herself at her own pace.

"Tonight was to be the culmination of those tests," she continued. "Your final exam I suppose you might say."

"And the purpose?" Hunt asked, causing a momentary flicker of annoyance to appear on Eve's face. She recovered quickly, however.

"I want you to join me, John." She stopped pacing and faced him head on. "I want you by my side."

"Why?"

Eve broke away from his gaze, looking at the ground. Hunt held his breath. Instinctively he knew this was the moment of truth. The point where he would get the answers he was looking for. When Eve looked back at him, her face had softened, returning to the stunning seductress he had become used to.

"Is it not enough for me to want you at my side?" She almost pleaded. "For me to want you to love and cherish every moment with me?"

Hunt sighed with disappointment. The answers had not been forthcoming. The disappointment formed a bitter taste in his mouth, but he had no time to consider things further as he detected movement in the corridor to his right.

Robed figures had broken the circle allowing access to the room from that corridor. Passing through the gap was a large, solid looking wooden table, wheeled in on castors by two more robed patrons. Following close behind the small group was Mr. Bera. He remained at the corridor entrance, outside of the circle, while the table was wheeled into the center of the room, coming to a gentle stop alongside Hunt and Eve.

The table was what caught Hunt's attention, more accurately, what was on it. The girl he had witnessed earlier being carried into the Exodus lay upon its smooth hard surface. The clothing she had been wearing now replaced by the same plain, white robe worn by the majority gathered in the room.

The last time he had seen the girl she was unconscious, but not now. Now she writhed and struggled against leather bindings securing her wrists and ankles to the table. A leather strap also secured her forehead. The leather gag, which had been forced into her mouth muffled her screams, but just barely.

As the table got closer, Hunt judged her age. She couldn't be more than fourteen. Just a child. Judging by the look in her eyes, she was terrified. Hunt looked at Eve, anger making his face flush.

"What is this?" he demanded. "Let her go!" Eve shook her head, slowly.

"I can't do that John. She is your final test."

Hunt looked confused. When the realization hit him, the confusion turned to outrage.

"You expect me to have sex with this girl?"

Immediately, the young girl's panic rose, and her struggles against her bindings increased. Eve smiled and began walking toward one of the two men who had wheeled the young girl into the room.

"No John," she replied with amusement. "This young creature has never known a man. Her purity is the reason she is here."

With her back to Hunt, he was unable to see the exchange between Eve and the man before her. He was taken aback when she turned holding both her hands out, palms up, a black stone dagger lying heavily across them.

It was a real work of art. Carved from a single piece of jet black stone that glowed with an inner light. The blade was triangular in shape, and both of its edges looked razor sharp. Etched into the blade and hilt, and picked out in silver leaf, was an intricate design which held no meaning for Hunt. He looked from the dagger to Eve, his face questioning.

"I need you to release her from this world, John. She must give her life so the Flame of Ephesus can burn for another generation."

"You want me to…" the words were still difficult to fathom, let alone say, "kill her?" Hunt was horrified.

Eve moved quickly toward him, her face intent. She grabbed his right arm at the wrist and thrust the hilt of the dagger into his hand. Her voice was an urgent whisper.

"Release her, John. Let the flame go on, and take your rightful place at my side."

There was a brief moment, as Hunt looked into Eve's eyes. The passion. The urgency. The need. He wavered. Her touch, her gaze, they had power over him, he realized. It was all too easy to succumb to her offer. A lifetime with Eve at his side. The temptation was real.

Hunt looked at the young girl, bound, gagged, and terrified. Tears were running down the side of her soft face into glistening pools on the wooden table. She was so young, innocent, full of life. Was he actually willing to pay that price? Take a child's life? Destroy everything she could be?

Hunt was well aware of his faults. He was not a particularly good or kind man. He was arrogant, self-centered, and selfish. But even considering this so-called offer disgusted him in ways he found difficult to put into words. Even with all his faults, there was a limit. He stared at Eve, his face like stone.

"No!" He cried with determination, thrusting the dagger back into her hands, and pushing her away from himself.

He derived a certain amount of satisfaction at the shocked look on Eves' face. It was evident she was not used to hearing that word, and for a moment she wasn't sure how to respond to it. Then her face hardened, eyes turning to sapphire shards of ice.

"You ungrateful fool," she spat vehemently. She turned and walked away, circling to the far side of the table so the girl lay between them. "Do you think you can save this girl?" She asked, her tone mocking. "Her life was forfeit from the moment she was born. You had a chance to join me, to stand at my side, to indulge in pleasures such as you have never dreamed of, and you give all that up, for this?"

Eve was gesticulating wildly with the knife in her hand. She was incensed, and Hunt feared not only for the girl's life but his own. She turned her back on him, raising her arms high and wide above her head.

"Loyal followers of the flame," she called in a loud voice, addressing the ring of spectators. "You have all heard Mr. Hunt's decision. He will not do what is required to ensure the survival of the Sacred Flame."

There was an angry murmuring from the gathered throng, and for a moment, Hunt feared they might all set upon him.

"Who among you will take his place and complete the ritual?"

"I will!" It was a female voice coming from behind Hunt.

He turned to see Julianna standing defiantly before him.

"You don't have to do this," he whispered urgently.

"You don't understand," she answered with barely concealed contempt.

"Come, child," Eve called encouragingly, as Julianna stepped past Hunt and around the head of the table to take her place by Eve's side.

Julianna's eyes were wild with excitement and anticipation as she took the stone dagger from Eve's outstretched hand.

"Stop!" Hunt cried desperately. "This is madness!"

He was just about to make a move to stop Julianna when four strong hands grabbed his arms. The two guards had moved from their positions flanking the candle, they now stood on either side of Hunt. Each had his arm in a vice-like grip holding him fast.

"Please, don't do this!"

Neither woman paid him any heed. Hunt watched in horror as Julianna stepped forward, closer to the table on which the young girl lay. He watched the child's face as the dagger was raised high above her. Her futile struggles intensified, her eyes going wide. She looked toward him imploringly.

"With this life," Julianna intoned, her voice loud and firm. "I grant life everlasting to the Sacred Flame. May it forever burn."

Hunt was watching the girl's expression as the knife fell. It pierced skin and bone with ease, slicing directly through to her heart. Her expression showed a brief moment of intense pain, her body arching in response to the brutal attack. She relaxed.

Her eyes never left Hunt. He saw the life leave her, as her blood flowed freely across the wooden table and onto the floor. In an instant, those bright, tearful and terrified eyes had become dull, cold and accusing in death. It was done.

Hunt sagged in defeat. Had he not been supported by the two guards he would have collapsed to the ground. Tears flowed freely down his face. The young girl was dead, and he had been unable to do anything to stop it from happening.

A hushed silence fell over the room in the aftermath of the girl's murder. The soft, regular drip, drip of the young girl's blood as it fell to the gradually expanding pool on the floor reverberated in the silence. It provided an accusatory counterpoint to the deep, racking sobs from Hunt.

"It is done," Eve intoned, her voice echoing hollowly. Hunt looked up his tear-streaked face a mask of pain and revulsion.

"Why?" He asked hoarsely.

Eve glanced across at him, viewing him much as one might inspect a cockroach, her face full of loathing. She turned towards Mr. Bera, who had remained in the corridor during the entire sequence of events.

"Remove him from my sight." She ordered coldly.

He inclined his head slightly in mute response as he glanced toward the guards still holding Hunt, and clicked his fingers.

The guards understood the signal. Half lifting, half dragging Hunt, they escorted him from the room. He provided little resistance. With the death of the young girl, Hunt's will had also died.

He blamed himself for her death. His arrogance, selfishness, and over-confidence, those were the reasons she now lay cooling on that table top. He had been so focused on finding his own "answers" he had barely given more than a cursory consideration of the girl's welfare. Had he gone to the police the first moment he saw her then, perhaps, this could have been avoided. But he had not. Her blood was on his hands, and it carried with it a stain on his soul that he did not think he could ever remove.

With Mr. Bera silently leading the way, the guards escorted Hunt back to the storeroom where he had been held previously. They tossed him unceremoniously into the room where he fell to his knees and stayed there. Mr. Bera stood in the doorway, watching him for a moment.

"I always knew it would come to this," he said, his voice devoid of emotion.

Hunt looked up at him as Mr. Bera reached into the inner folds of his jacket and produced a small revolver.

"You're going to kill me?" Hunt asked in a hoarse voice. It was more of a statement than a question.

Bera shrugged. "We can't very well let you go now, can we Mr. Hunt?"

Hunt's head dropped. He knew he was supposed to be afraid, but he was not. After what he had just witnessed, death no longer held any fear for him. In truth, he felt it was no more than he deserved.

He remained kneeling, face down, staring at the floor. There was no fight left, no will to live. All he wanted now was an end to the pain and guilt.

Hunt paid no heed as Mr. Bera raised the pistol, aimed it, point blank at his head, and fired.

Chapter 20

Eve was disappointed. The evening had not gone as she had hoped. Hunt's refusal to bow to her will had both annoyed and deeply upset her. Despite the fact that the sacrifice had still gone ahead, she remained in an irritable mood.

Julianna, however, was in her element. She had always been a highly sexual, and somewhat perverse creature, but the events of the evening so far had escalated her inborn desires to new heights. The murder of the young girl had stoked a fire within Julianna that was now burning out of control. She had stripped out of her robe as fast as she could, exposing her lush form to everyone gathered. Anointing herself with the girl's blood Julianna had then allowed herself to be passed from person to person to be used as they saw fit. This had rapidly turned into an orgiastic frenzy with her, a willing participant at its heart.

Eve was standing to one side of the mass of writhing, moaning bodies, observing dispassionately. Ordinarily, she would have been heavily involving herself in this element of the activities, but not tonight. She remained fully robed and vaguely distracted.

Mr. Bera approached with a certain degree of wariness, his two burly guards in tow. He had known Eve for a very long time and had developed excellent instincts regarding her capricious nature. This would not be a good time to irritate her further. She turned toward him as he neared her.

"Is it done?" She asked shortly.

He nodded, motioning for the guards to continue on into the main area of the club.

"It was necessary," he stated.

"I am well aware of that!" She snapped. She took a deep breath to calm herself before continuing. "I felt so sure this time. How could I have been so wrong?"

There was nothing Bera could say to this that would not arouse her ire, so he remained silent. Eve, meanwhile, questioned why Hunt had been sent to her. There must have been some purpose to his presence, she thought, but whatever that purpose had been, had ended with his death. Such a waste. She shook her head in confusion.

"You should go and make sure the rest of our guests are happy," Eve ordered.

Bera nodded. "Of course Eve. I have a cleanup crew standing by. As soon as we finish here tonight, they can come and dispose of, everything."

"Thank you, Bera."

Bera bowed his head in acknowledgment and headed off toward the corridor that led to the main Club area.

Chapter 21

A fresh cool breeze blew through the trees, rustling the leaves and creating a gentle whispering that was somehow comforting. Nearby a small brook gurgled and babbled excitedly, it's clear, fresh water sparkling in the bright sunshine. Overhead, joyous songbirds sang a musical medley, a testament to happier times. All around was the scent of crisp, green grass and wildflowers, an altogether intoxicating aroma, full of promise and life. The area held an overriding air of peace and tranquility.

All of this came as something of a surprise to Hunt as he cautiously opened his eyes, blinking in the bright sunlight. The last thing he could remember was the split second of searing pain as the bullet struck him in his left temple, then, nothing.

He moved his head gently from side to side, taking in the idyllic scene around him. What is this place? He wondered.

"You're awake, I see."

Hunt jumped involuntarily at the sound of the voice that had so rudely intruded upon such a tranquil moment. He sat up quickly, looking around him in a slight panic. He let out a shocked gasp when he finally located the voice's owner.

"I was beginning to think you were going to sleep the day away," Andrew remarked in a voice thick with sarcasm.

Hunt sat stock still, mouth open in mute shock. Before him, sitting casually on a medium-sized, gray stone was Andrew. That was surprising in its own right, but what was even more surprising was his appearance. This was Andrew as Hunt remembered him, fit, healthy, no sign of the injuries he had suffered as a result of the mortar strike. How was this possible?

"Well, are you just going to sit there, or are you going to come and grab some food?"

Hunt realized what he had at first taken to be a mere stone was actually a roughly carved stool. There was a second such stool opposite Andrew, currently empty, and between the two was a small, carved stone table upon which a variety of wooden bowls rested.

As Hunt watched Andrew plucking some form of lush looking red berries from one of the bowls and popping them into his mouth, he realized that he was indeed hungry. Actually ravenous would have been a better description. Hunt rose slowly, cautiously and made his way towards the stone seat, drawn by the hypnotic sights and smells of the fresh food.

"Do you know, you snore?" Andrew quizzed as Hunt made himself comfortable on the stool. "Sounds like a bloody freight train. You've been scaring all the wildlife away."

"Where am I?" Hunts' voice was a mix of wonder and confusion.

"That's always the first question," Andrew observed cryptically. "We can talk while you eat."

Hunt needed no further urging. The bowls were filled with an assortment of colorful, fresh fruits, berries and tasty looking nuts. Hunt began eating with a passion, marveling at the taste explosion in his mouth. Andrew watched him with a slight smile.

"So, you're wondering where you are," Andrew continued as John ate. "It's probably easiest to think of this place as a stepping stone."

"A stepping stone to what?" Hunt asked between mouthfuls.

"Not to," Andrew corrected. "A stepping stone betweenyour life on Earth and what comes next."

"So I am dead then?"

Andrew shook his head. "That's not as easy to answer as you might think," he declared.

"From where I sit, it's not all that complex," John held up his hand. He mimicked the action of firing a gun at his own temple. "A gunshot to the head has a certain ring of finality to it," he remarked, flatly.

"Ordinarily, I would agree," Andrew admitted. "But there is nothing ordinary about this, and there is nothing ordinary about you. You are…"

"Unique!" John interrupted, hotly. "You know. I'm a little tired of hearing that. Ever since I got out of the hospital, I've had every man and his dog tell me how unique I am, but no one wants to say what that means."

"Calm down," Andrew reassured soothingly.

"I'll calm down when I start getting some straight answers."

"No one could give you answers, John because they did not know or, as was the case with me, the time wasn't right."

"And is this the right time?"

"Yes," Andrew responded.

Hunt had not expected that. He paused, taking a deep breath, visibly calming himself before looking back up at Andrew.

"Fine," he retorted finally. "I'm listening."

"First, I need to ask you, do you want to die?"

Hunt was shocked at the stupidity of the question, but then as the thought sunk in, he realized it wasn't really all that stupid after all. He considered his life, in particular, the events of the last week. He hadn't covered himself in glory, he realized, with no small amount of shame. He had not led the best life, and he could not claim that his life had been joyous. So what would be the point in continuing? No-one would miss him.

Andrew watched with interest as a range of emotions passed across Hunt's face.

"Well?" Andrew pressed finally.

"No" he answered, defiantly. "Of course, I don't."

Ultimately, the decision came down to one consideration. As bad as his life may have been, if there was any chance to improve it, to be a better person, he wanted it. Plain and simple. Andrew nodded in apparent understanding.

"And, if given the chance," Andrew prompted, "what would you do with it?"

This required almost no thought. Hunt's mind instantly replayed the final moments before he was shot. He saw the terrified face of the innocent girl as she was impaled through the heart. As the memory repeated over and over in his mind, Hunt gazed at Andrew, his face like stone.

"I would stop Eve," he announced with grim determination. "I would make her pay for what she has done."

"Vengeance?" Andrew asked curiously.

No," Hunt replied, flatly. "Justice."

"As good a reason as any," Andrew conceded. He studied Hunt's face carefully before continuing. "Consider yourself fortunate. You have the power to return, should you so choose."

"I don't understand," Hunt confessed.

"Let me tell you a story," Andrew started, his voice soft, yet serious. "At the beginning of time, when mankind was first created all men were given the power of choice. I am not talking about the simple act of self-determination, the ability to direct one's own life. I am speaking about actual power. The power to choose when you die."

"Immortality?"

"Of a sort, yes," Andrew confirmed. "At that time there was no such thing as a natural aging process. People grew up, grew old and died, all at a pace of their own choosing. Unfortunately, for reasons I will not go into now, that power was stripped away, leaving mankind with only the uncertainty surrounding life and death. And so it continues to this day. "You are unique, John, for reasons I cannot explain. For you, the whole concept of life and death has been reduced to a simple choice."

Hunt didn't know what to say. The implications inherent in what Andrew was telling him were just too huge to immediately grasp. Ordinarily, Hunt would have scoffed at such a notion, his current position, however, made the message, absurd as it may have sounded, far harder to dismiss. He knew he had been shot in the head, he remembered it, he felt it still, yet here he was, having this conversation. If that were possible, then why should he not believe what he had just been told. If this were indeed true, and this incredible power was his to command, then there was still one important question outstanding.

"Why me?" Hunt asked suspiciously.

"Because you are needed," Andrew answered, vaguely. He could see that Hunt wanted more. "That is all I can say. Right now you need to decide what happens next."

"You're serious," Hunt said sourly. "You mean, I still get a choice in this?"

"Of course. Choice lies at the core of everything, John. You can choose to ignore all I have said and continue on your natural way, wherever that may lead, or, you may decide to return and set right a few wrongs. It is entirely up to you."

"I'm going back," Hunt declared. He knew what he needed to do. There was a reckoning to be had with a woman named, Eve. Hunt's stony face suddenly softened, he almost looked embarrassed.

"Just one question. How do I do it?"

Andrew laughed. It was a pleasant sound that finally made Hunt relax a little.

"The choice is a conscious act, much like choosing to move a limb. Close your eyes, concentrate on what you want."

"That's it?" Hunt asked doubtfully. Andrew nodded.

"Before you go, John," Andrew said. "I have to warn you, most of what has happened here you will forget. These are not the kind of memories one can carry into the living world. There are two things I need you to remember."

"Oh?" John grunted, his suspicions growing once more. "You have been given power over the life force woven throughout the fabric of your world. Be careful how you use it."

Hunt nodded thoughtfully. "And the second?"

"No gift of this magnitude comes without a price or purpose. When we next meet, you will learn both."

"I see," Hunt scowled, looking around slowly. There was a taint of sadness in his eyes as he realized this was the most peaceful place he had ever seen. There would be no such beauty where he was going. He looked at Andrew, who looked sympathetic as if he knew what Hunt was feeling.

"It's time," Andrew murmured.

Hunt nodded, and forcing himself to relax, closed his eyes and concentrated.

Looking back at this moment, Hunt would never quite be sure what happened next. There was momentary darkness, followed by disorientation. He wanted to vomit. Before it all turned black, he thought he heard a voice. It was Andrew. His voice was faint as if carried over a great distance. Two words…

"I'm sorry."

Chapter 22

It had been a long night, but it was gradually drawing to a close. Eve's guests had partaken of every pleasure imaginable, all under her ever watchful gaze. Now a mass of naked bodies lay before her, sighing in the contented afterglow of their sexual marathon.

While she could feel the waves of pleasure and contentment emanating from the bodies arrayed before her, Eve did not share those feelings. Her mood remained pensive, irritable. Hunt's earlier refusal had successfully tainted everything that followed. Were he still alive, she would have considered killing him again out of pure spite.

"EVE!" The loud, guttural cry made everyone pause.

All eyes turned toward the source. Many the females screamed in terror, one of them fainting. The men just stared, open-mouthed, rooted in fear. Upon seeing the apparition standing in the room, Eve turned to Bera, but he was gone. In disgust, Eve turned back to face the gruesome apparition. Hunt was standing, barely, just inside the room. It had taken all of his willpower to make it that far. Andrew neglected to mention he would be returned to his body in the same condition he had left it.

A gunshot wound to the head has a tendency to cause a lot of damage. In Hunt's case, this meant he had opened his eyes, or at least one of them, to find a significant portion of the right side of his head spread across the floor. The pain was beyond description. Every nerve ending was on fire and movement of any kind was like pouring gasoline on the flames.

Hunt was driven by intense need, a hunger he couldn't quite define, but one he had to satisfy. As he stood, in front of all of those terrified people, it was that insatiable hunger driving him forward. Many the patrons scattered in terror at his approach, while the rest remained paralyzed in their fear.

Eve watched in fascination as Hunt neared the closest patron, a young woman, curled into a quivering ball. Her arms were covering her head, she didn't see his approach. Hunt reached out and laid a hand on her bare shoulder.

The instant his hand made contact, she screamed and tried to pull away, but he held her fast. Hunt felt the change immediately, the sudden burst of energy flowing up his arm and into his body making him gasp in surprise. The girl before him arched her back in pain, the scream of terror becoming a rasping gurgle. Her eyes began to grow dim, and the color slowly left her body. All the while Hunt could feel strength and vitality flowing through him.

As his strength returned, so did his reason. Andrew's parting words flooded his mind, *"...you have been given power over the life force woven throughout the fabric of your world..."*

Hunt understood exactly what was happening. He was stealing this young woman's life energy, taking it for himself.

Suddenly, the flow of energy stopped. He looked down. The girl was little more than a grayed husk. He released her in disgust.

Eve had watched as events unfolded before her, but as the young woman slumped to the floor with a dull thud, her expression changed to one of outrage.

"No!" She breathed. "That is not possible!"

Hunt, meanwhile, had moved on. The life force he had stolen had given him renewed energy. His strength was returning, his vision clearing and the pain was beginning to lessen. His body was using the stolen energy to repair itself. He could feel the tissues gradually reforming, bone and flesh growing and knitting together at a remarkable rate. He was repulsed at what was happening, at the same time he was powerless to resist the forces currently acting upon him. He was being driven by instinct and need, the hunger pushing him on to further acts of gruesome theft. Leaving the girl behind him, Hunt now had a man in his clutches, gripping his head with both hands, maintaining eye contact as he feasted upon the life energy.

The two burly guards who had left the room earlier, at Mr. Bera's instruction, chose that moment to return. They entered at a run, coming to a sudden stop as they beheld the strange sight before them.

At least half of the VIP patrons had passed them in the corridor as they stampeded, naked into the main Club area, causing no small panic. As a result of this the guards had expected something, but what they were faced with was so bizarre, they struggled to comprehend it.

Hunt rose up from the second grayed corpse. His injuries had virtually healed now, and the instinctive hunger had lessened to the point where he felt in marginal control of himself. He knew he still needed to feast, but he no longer wished to be so indiscriminate about his choice of victim. As much as he felt everyone in the room deserved to die, there were two, in particular, he wanted to find. Eve and Julianna.

Scanning the few remaining patrons, it was clear that Julianna had the good sense to run at the earliest opportunity, but Eve, she remained, watching him from across the room. With grim determination, Hunt began walking towards her. Those patrons that had remained, cowering in fear, saw an opportunity to make their escape. Hunt ignored them as they scampered away, skirting past Eve and the two guards.

The guards looked unsure of what to do, neither looked comfortable with tackling Hunt. The last memory they had of him involved him lying on the ground in an expanding pool of his own blood and brains. In their experience, people did not usually get up and walk away from something like that, never mind embarking upon some bizarre, murderous rampage. Eve glanced at them, instructing them with a single look to take the initiative.

This put the guards in a bit of a quandary, and they struggled for a moment trying to decide which of the two, Eve or Hunt, they feared the most.

Hunt noted their indecision, but something else as well. He was now suffused with life energy, and as a result, his healing was virtually complete. He was clear-headed, lucid, but his vision had changed. He could detect a faint, wispy glow around the bodies of the guards and the fleeing patrons. He held his own hand up to examine it and realized the glow surrounded himself as well, although his glow was much brighter. It took him a moment to understand what he was looking at. His vision had altered in a way that allowed him to see the energy that existed in all living things.

Engrossed in this new discovery, Hunt did not notice the approach of one of the guards. On seeing that Hunt was distracted the larger of the two guards had decided to avail himself of the unexpected opportunity and had charged.

It was not until the man was only a stride away that Hunt finally noted the danger. Acting purely on instinct, his left arm shot out, hand catching the startled guard by the throat. To the guard this was like running into a wall, it stopped him cold. As before, the instant Hunt's hand connected, his body began to feast. Hunt watched in rapt fascination as he could now see the life energy transferring from the guard to himself, his own aura growing measurably brighter with each passing second.

The second guard had remained undecided until this point.

Now, seeing his companion dying before his eyes, he made a decision that was based purely upon survival. He turned and ran, much to the disgust of Eve.

Eve turned to watch the guard scurry along the corridor before turning back just in time to see Hunt releasing the second guard, yet another grayed husk. As the guard landed heavily at his feet, Hunt studied Eve. Throughout all of this, she had remained in the room, unafraid. Despite himself, Hunt was impressed by the level of her composure. But as he studied her now, there was something else that captured his attention more than her bravery. His newly acquired sight could see the life force around everyone he had thus far encountered, yet from Eve it saw nothing. There was not the barest trace of an aura. Before he had the time to ponder this puzzle she stepped forward, smiling that slow, seductive smile that he had come to know so well these past few days.

"Have you come back to me John?" she cooed, almost playfully.

"Only to kill you," Hunt answered.

"You could still take your place by my side."

"I don't think so."

By now Eve was directly in front of him, looking straight up at his bloodied face. There was no hint of fear in her expression. She held her wrists up to him.

"Well then I suppose you have to kill me," she teased sweetly.

Without pause Hunt took a rough hold on both of her wrists, all the while maintaining eye contact. He wanted to watch those sapphire pools dim and fade as he drew the life force out of her. But nothing happened. The seconds ticked by and she remained unharmed, her smile broadening as his confusion grew.

"Oh my poor boy," she taunted. "Is it really so hard to understand?"

Hunt pushed her away, releasing her and turning away in disgust.

"What are you?" he demanded.

"I am like you John, unique."

"You are nothing like me!" he screamed, walking away from her. What he needed now more than anything was distance. "You're a murderer."

"Perhaps I am John." She admitted. "But I see four bodies in this room, and only one of them has anything to do with me. So, you tell me, who is the murderer?"

"I had no choice." It sounded lame, even to Hunt's own ears.

"Neither did I."

"Why?" Hunt demanded. "Why was it necessary to kill an innocent young girl?"

"The Flame," Eve answered simply.

Hunt turned to look at the large candle. It was evident he did not understand.

"Why is this flame so important?" he asked.

Eve shook her head, a look of profound sadness on her face.

"You have been told nothing have you?" She marveled. "I pity you, John. That is the Flame of Ephesus. It is a mystical, everlasting fire that must never be allowed to dim. Once each generation a sacrifice is required to maintain the fire. The sacrifice must be a virgin. My existence has one purpose, to maintain the flame."

Hunt had barely been listening to Eve. His attention had been captured by the candle and its mystical flame. The moment he looked at it, his new vision had shown him the truth of Eves' words. The candle, the flame, they produced an aura, they had a life force. The aura was strong, stronger than anything he had thus far encountered. As Eve explained the purpose of the sacrifice, Hunt understood. Somehow, the sacrificial act had allowed the life force to be transferred from the young girl to the candle, which in turn provided the flame with everlasting life.

While Eve had been talking, Hunt had moved to within reach of the flame. An idea had been forming in his head, but he needed to know more.

"So your sole purpose has been to maintain this flame?" He asked without turning around.

"Yes."

"And how long have you been doing this?"

"For as long as I can remember," Eve answered.

"I see."

As Hunt studied the aura around the candle, he wondered how many sacrifices had been required to make it so bright. How many young, innocent virgins? How much blood? He knew what he needed to do.

"Eve?" He murmured, his right hand slowly reaching out to the candle. There was something about his tone that caught her attention. She looked at him suspiciously.

"What are you doing John?" She asked, and for the first time Hunt detected a hint of fear in her voice.

"I think it's time you were released from that burden," Hunt responded, placing his hand against the cold surface of the candle.

The moment Eve realized what he intended to do she launched herself towards him, but she was too far away.

"Nooo!" she cried in anguish.

The shock as the life energy from the candle poured into him was staggering, he gasped in surprise, nearly losing his grip on the smooth wax. This was nothing like the energies he had thus far stolen. They were tainted and weak, but this, the pure force of countless innocents, was sweet and vibrant, it made every nerve tingle with pleasure.

Hunt lost all awareness of his surroundings, overtaken by the ecstasy of the moment. He did not notice that Eve had taken him by his free arm and was trying, with all her might, to pull him away from the candle. She screamed at him in desperation and exerted all her strength in a futile attempt to pry him loose.

The energy continued to course through Hunt. It filled every pore of his being; his very cells pulsed with the sheer power of it. His entire being was filled to capacity so that he glowed with a radiant inner light, both beautiful and terrible to behold. Still, the energy flowed.

Hunt gasped in sudden alarm. He could feel that his body had reached its capacity, and now was threatening to explode under the strain of containing even more. He wanted to pull away, but despite every ounce of concentration he could muster, he could not release his grip, and the energy continued to flow.

As Hunt looked around him, desperately searching for a way to release the destructive force building inside, he became aware of Eve. She was still struggling to pull him away from the candle. Seeing her there, so close to him, his arm reached out of its own volition. Instinctively he knew this was the right, and only course of action.

The instant his hand touched her chest it was like a floodgate had been opened. The life force he had been struggling so hard to contain was released. Hunt was no longer a container for the energy rather he had become a conduit, a highway, allowing it free passage directly into Eve. She stopped fighting with him the moment the transfer began. Her eyes bulged from their sockets in shock, while her mouth dropped open in a silent scream.

As the life energy traveled from the candle, through Hunt and into Eve, he began to understand what had happened earlier when he had tried to destroy Eve as he had destroyed the others. He had been unable to siphon the life force from Eve for the simple reason that she had none to give. She was empty and hollow. He had no idea how she had managed to survive without any life energy, but it was clear that she had found a way. Now that Hunt needed to offload the energy coming from the candle, she provided the perfect receptacle, and the energy filled the void within her.

As the life force filled her being, however, Eve's struggles to break free became even more frantic. She screamed as if she were being burned alive. This Hunt did not immediately understand. But Eve knew only too well. She knew that she had no hope of containing the energies she was now receiving. Her form had survived for so long without the existence of a life force that it was no longer capable of holding the one it was now being given. Her entire being was being torn apart, piece by piece, by the forces tearing through her.

Without warning, it stopped. The energy ceased to flow from the candle. The flame flickered and died. As Hunt tried to release his grip, he realized the wax had become dry and brittle. The candle collapsed in on itself, becoming little more than a pile of dust.

Although Hunt still contained a painful amount of energy, he had successfully transferred a significant portion of it to Eve. As he looked at her now, he realized that she had no hope of containing that energy for much longer. Her smooth, alabaster skin had become gray and brittle with age, her hair had turned white, and had lost its glossy sheen. She looked up at him imploringly through silver- grey eyes. Where once she had been young and beautiful now she was impossibly ancient.

The absence of life had caused the candle to age and die. For Eve it was much the same. She had survived so long without life that now the presence of it in such massive quantities had caused her to age at a frightening rate. She was dying right before his eyes. With her final breath and in a cracked and breaking voice she said one word to Hunt.

"Why?"

Her eyes dimmed, and she crumpled to the ground, lifeless and still. Hunt's extended vision allowed him to see the life energy escaping into the world as her body was no longer able to contain it. Looking down at the crumpled form, there was only one answer he could give.

"Because I had no choice."

Chapter 23

Hunt looked around the now silent room, surveying his handiwork. Four bodies lay on the floor, all killed by his hand. His focus, however, was drawn to the fifth, the pale remains of the young girl, a gaping wound above her heart where the stone dagger had pierced her so cruelly. She was still bound and gagged. Hunt could no longer bear to see her that way, trussed up like a slab of meat, he could feel the anger rising at the sight of her. There had to be some form of dignity in death, especially a death as pointless as this one.

He walked over to the table where she lay and began undoing her bonds, hands shaking with anger, making the task more difficult. This was more than just anger Hunt was also wracked with guilt and profound sorrow. He should have been able to do something more, he should have been able to prevent this from happening. At least he had made those responsible, pay for what they had done.

He removed the leather gag last, being as gentle as possible. As he saw the young face in its entirety for the first time, his eyes began to swell with tears of sorrow. She was once a pretty girl before life had left its cruel, abusive mark upon her. He had a sudden urge to just pick her up and carry her out of that horrible, death-laden room. He had enough surplus energy. He could probably carry her halfway around the world before tiring.

Pausing, his brain re-ran that last thought. He had complete control of life energy. He had proven that already this evening. So far he had only used that control to destructive ends. He knew, however, that he could do more than steal energy from people. He had given Eve a portion of the life force he had stolen from the candle.

She had been unable to contain it. Her form had not held the light of life for so long it had lost the ability to make use of it. This young girl was different. Up until only a short time ago, she had been a young, vibrant, living being. Hunt knew that what he was considering was outrageous, and probably outside of many scientific, and most likely religious laws. He figured he had already broken enough of them already, what harm could he really do now? Before he could talk himself out of it, he placed a hand upon the girl's chest and concentrated.

The life force began to flow almost immediately. Hunt could see it leaving his hand and entering the still form of the young girl. In truth Hunt had no idea what he was doing, he was operating on intuition, guesswork, and more than a little hope.

A minute passed in agonizing slowness. Hunt was maintaining a steady, controlled flow of energy and carefully monitoring the girl for any response. There was none, not even the merest flicker. By now he had relinquished almost all of the life force stolen from the candle. If he continued, he would have no choice but to give his own life force in the attempt.

"Come on," he whispered desperately. "Come back, please!"

Still no response. Hunt was becoming weaker now. He knew he would not be able to continue for much longer before he passed out from exhaustion. He dropped to one knee, gripping the edge of the table with his free hand for additional support.

Hunt had reached the point of no return. If he did not stop now, then he risked killing himself in the attempt. There was still no response from the young girl. He pulled his hand away, breaking the connection, slumping to a crumpled seated position, leaning against a leg of the table.

He felt drained and broken; rivers of tears ran down his face as he repeated two words over and over to anyone who may have been listening.

"I'm sorry."

Hunt would never really know how long he sat there, apologizing to a young girl who would never hear him. Eventually, though, he did regain some measure of composure. Rising on unsteady legs, Hunt gave one last regretful look towards the young girl before leaving the room.

He stumbled his way along the corridor, occasionally leaning against the side wall to remain upright. It was evident long before he reached it, that the main club was empty. The music was off, and while the lights were on, they remained still and fixed. Obviously, Mr. Bera and his cronies decided that retreat was the safest course of action. This suited him just fine. At this point, Hunt had little idea of where he was going or what he was going to do, but only the Gods could help anyone he met tonight who had any connection to Club Exodus.

Hunt moved unsteadily across the dance floor toward the bar. It may not have been the most sensible thing to do at this point, but he needed a drink, and he felt they probably owed him at least one 'on the house'.

He passed through the open bar hatch and began searching behind the counter, feeling reasonably confident that they would have a good supply of his favorite drinks, based on the level of knowledge they had displayed so far. It took only a few moments to find what he was looking for, two fresh, unopened bottles of sixteen-year-old Lagavulin, single malt whisky. He took both, also collecting a 'waiter's friend' on the way back out from behind the counter. The waiter's friend was a simple tool, much like a basic pocket knife in design. It had a small knife and a corkscrew that both folded away, discretely into the handle. It was the knife Hunt was using now, peeling away the outer wrapping from the top of one of the bottles as he continued on to the main entrance.

It was early morning by the time Hunt left the building. He figured he must have been one hell of a sight, face still soaked with blood, two bottles of potent spirits in his hands, drinking straight from the neck of one of them.

He stood at the open gates at the edge of the factory compound with no idea where to go next. Tilting his head back, he took a long slug of whisky, allowing the smoky flavor to fill his mouth, before releasing its warmth into his throat, feeling it flow through his body.

Hunt was considering his options when he noticed a figure standing in the shadows of a tree across the road from him. He recognized the dark shape immediately and began walking across the road toward him. The fact that the figure was standing in almost the exact same spot John himself had used to observe the compound the previous day did not escape his notice. Coincidence? He didn't think so.

"You're a bit late, Andrew," Hunt remarked sullenly as he joined his former cameraman in the dark, early morning shadows. "The party's over."

"I'd guessed as much," Andrew stated. "So what are you doing now? Drowning your sorrows?"

"Seemed like a good idea," Hunt noted, sitting on the grass and leaning back against the trunk of the tree.

Andrew watched him as he took another drink from the open bottle.

"It won't do any good you know," he advised.

Hunt grunted and took another gulp of the dark brown liquid almost as an act of defiance. Andrew sighed, sitting down next to him against the tree. For a few moments they remained that way, neither saying anything.

"Why is this happening to me?" Hunt asked.

"Because it is supposed to."

"What the hell does that mean?" Hunt demanded.

"Everybody in this world has a purpose," Andrew chose his words cautiously and spoke softly. "Most don't realize it, or don't think about it. They just go through their everyday lives, completely unaware of the fact that they are fulfilling some little goal somewhere, some infinitesimal act within that grand drama which they call life. Usually, they have no awareness of the task even when it is being fulfilled, but on very rare occasions someone is expected to fulfill a much greater purpose."

"And is that what I am doing here? Performing some great task?" Andrew nodded. "Then I'm done, right? I'm finished?"

"I'm afraid you have barely begun John," Andrew answered softly. "This was just one small step on the road that now lies before you."

"But I don't know what I'm doing!" Hunt cried. "There are five people dead in there, and I don't know why!" He gestured wildly towards the derelict factory compound.

"I understand that John, but…"

"I killed them, Andrew!" Hunt interrupted. "Those people are dead because of me! I have to be able to make some kind of sense of that!"

Hunt was virtually pleading now. Andrew could see the desperation and the guilt that was etched into Hunt's face.

"Three people were killed by your hand John, and all of them deserved their fate. The fourth, the young girl, you had nothing to do with her death. You could not have stopped it. As for the fifth, well, I'm sure you've worked out by now that Eve was not entirely human."

"True," Hunt conceded. "But then, I'm not entirely human anymore am I?"

"An individual's humanity is not measured by how they look or what abilities they may or may not have. It is measured purely by what lies in their heart and soul."

"Really poetic Andrew, but as usual, you're avoiding my questions. What the hell was that all about in there?"

Andrew studied Hunt intently for a moment before answering. "The Flame of Ephesus."

"That damned candle?" Hunt asked. "What the hell was so important about a bit of wax?"

"You know as well as I do, that was no simple candle. That was an artifact of great power and influence. It needed to be destroyed."

Hunt nodded, remembering the events surrounding the eventual destruction of the candle. There was no denying that Andrew spoke the truth, yet there was something still missing.

"Why couldn't you just tell me that in the first place?" Hunt asked.

"I couldn't do that," Andrew stated. "Everything you have done these past few days, everything you have witnessed and experienced has been as a direct result of choices you have made. I could not directly influence those choices, if I had, the end results could have been very different."

"I see," Hunt said. "So the candle is gone, what happens now?"

"Now you rest," Andrew answered.

"That simple?"

"Of course."

Hunt stood slowly, thinking hard about what had just been said, and what had happened. Andrew watched him, sensing that something wasn't quite right. The look on

Hunt's face when he turned confirmed Andrew's suspicions. There was weariness there, a profound sorrow and guilt, but also defiance.

"No Andrew," Hunt murmured. "It's not that simple. I've been led around by the nose all week. Manipulated like some kind of puppet on a string. And why? So I could be your hatchet man, your assassin."

"You don't understand," Andrew stated.

"No, I don't. You're right. I don't understand any of this, and I don't want to. I never asked to become a part of this world, and I don't want anything more to do with it. You turned me into some kind of freakish monster and set me loose on some vague journey for God only knows what purpose. Well, I'm sorry Andrew, I'm nobody's puppet. We're done, you and I."

"What about the price?"

"There's five bodies back there and a busted candle!" Hunt snapped angrily, gesturing back towards the factory. "Consider it paid in full." Hunt took a long drink, draining the bottle in the process. He tossed it to the grass at Andrew's feet and began walking.

"Where are you going to go?" Andrew asked.

"Anywhere that's away from here," Hunt responded. He paused and turned back to face Andrew. "I don't want to see you again Andrew, understand?"

Andrew watched as Hunt turned away once more and continued walking.

"You of all people should know," he murmured, "we don't always get what we want in this world, John."

Epilogue

The VIP room of the Exodus was silent, the bodies remaining untouched, forgotten. That silence was rudely shattered by the heavy pounding of booted feet from the corridor that led from the main Club area. Mr. Bera entered, followed by two of his massive guards. He paused just inside the room.

Surveying the scene, he noted the grey-skinned bodies on the ground and the young girl still lying on the table. His attention was caught by the fact that her bonds had been removed. He moved across to the large, wheeled table and began a closer examination of the leather bindings that had held the girl in place.

A momentary surprise registered on his face as he saw that they were intact, showing visible signs of having been removed with some care. He fingered one of the leather straps absently.

"Such a sentimentalist Mr. Hunt," he murmured, softly.

Walking around the table, Bera noticed the remains of Eve for the first time. There was a sharp intake of breath as he noted the condition of her corpse. He moved closer and knelt on one knee to better examine her. He was reluctant to touch or even get too close to the desiccated form that had once been his mistress. As he viewed the results of Hunt's handiwork, he muttered to himself.

"My poor Eve. You had such high hopes for this one."

He rose, with some difficulty, back to his feet and turned to where the Flame of Ephesus once burned. Now there was little more than a sad looking pile of dust.

There was a commotion from the hallway. The two guards in the room looked around to see two more guards manhandling someone along the corridor. As they reached the entrance to the room, the man was pushed forward. He stumbled to his knees. Bera turned to look at him.

"Ah Carl," he said amiably. "My boys found you then."

This was the same guard who had attempted to ambush Hunt in the alley two nights ago. He looked up at Bera fearfully.

"You were supposed to kill Hunt," Bera remarked, pointedly.

"It was all that bitch's fault, Mr. Bera. She came out of nowhere, killed all of my boys. I was lucky to escape."

Carl rubbed his right arm absently as he said this, remembering the wounding he had received at the hands of Jane.

"Lucky?" Bera spat. "I should kill you for your failure." He swept an arm around the room. "This is your fault, Carl. Had you done your job, none of this would have happened."

"I'm sorry, Mr. Bera," Carl mumbled contritely. "Please, give me another chance."

Bera walked across the room toward Carl. "Strangely enough Carl, and against my better judgment, that is exactly what I intend to do. Stand!"

Carl did as commanded, towering at least a foot over the diminutive Bera. He looked down at his master, a glimmer of hope in his eyes.

"I'm going to give you a chance to redeem yourself. I don't care what you have to do. I don't care what it takes. You are going to find John Hunt."

Printed in January 2023
by Rotomail Italia S.p.A., Vignate (MI) - Italy